Geronimo Stilton

Thea Stilton
THE MAGIC OF
THE MIRROR

Scholastic Inc.

Library of Congress Cataloging-in-Publication Data available

ISBN 978-1-338-65509-4

Text by Thea Stilton
Original title *Lo specchio segreto delle fate*
Art director Iacopo Bruno
Illustrations by Guiseppe Facciotto, Barbara Pellizzari, Chiara Balleello, Valeria Brambilla, and Alessandro Muscillo
Graphics by Daria Colombo

Special thanks to AnnMarie Anderson
Translated by Anna Pizzelli
Interior design by Kay Petronio

10 9 8 7 6 5 4 3 2 1   20 21 22 23 24

Printed in China   62

First edition October, 2020

THE THEA SiSTERS

THEA

PAULINA

Colette

Violet

nicky

PAMELA

The Fantasy Worlds

Arvin is a mysterious knight who was banished from the fantasy kingdoms for breaking the rules.

Fuchsia is a Color Fairy. She is in love with Arvin, and her greatest dream is to be reunited with him one day.

Sigma is a leprechaun and the guardian of the Starlight Kingdom's Harmony. He lives underground on a silver planet where he welcomes visitors cheerfully.

Beryl is the fairy guardian of the Crystal Kingdom's Harmony. Red is her favorite color and the color of the precious stone beryl, for which she is named.

The Fairy of Good Counsel is the guardian of the Land of Flowers' Harmony. She knows a secret hiding place that is hidden from all who try to find it.

Aurita is a jellyfish and the guardian of the Harmony of Aquamarina, the Land of the Sea. She may look scary, but she is a gentle and kind creature.

Molton is a brave prince of the Kingdom of Nimbus. He saved Ariel, guardian of the Harmony in the Land of Clouds, from a stormy vortex.

The Kitsune Fairies are the guardians of the Land of Minwa's Harmony. They live in a rock palace where they sculpt beautiful crystal jewelry out of ice.

The Swamp Nymph is the guardian of the Land of Erin's Harmony. She lives in a tree in the middle of the swamp.

ART, NATURE, AND A MYSTERY

It was a warm spring morning at Mouseford Academy. The sun was on the horizon and birds chirped happily while flowers, still wet from the morning dew, opened their petals to the light of a new day.

"Good morning!" Violet called happily as she knocked on the door to Colette and Pamela's room.

Pamela sat up in bed, rubbing her eyes.

"Is it time to get up already?" she mumbled sleepily.

"Yes, it is!" Violet replied eagerly. "Paulina and I are going to the ART AND NATURE workshop. Do you want to come along?"

"What time is it?" Colette asked. She was also still in bed.

"It's eight o'clock," Paulina replied, popping her head into the room. "Three minutes before eight, to be exact."

"It's way too early!" Colette complained. "I just want to roll over and go back to sleep!"

"Then you'd miss out on painting in nature," Violet said. "It's so relaxing."

"Nicky's coming, too," Paulina added.

"Okay, okay," Pam groaned. "There's going to be breakfast there, right?"

"Of course!" Paulina reassured her. "There's an amazing buffet waiting for us!"

"In that case, I'll be dressed and ready to go in five minutes!" Pam exclaimed eagerly as she LEAPED out of her bed.

"What about you, Colette?" Violet asked. "Will you join us?"

Colette fell back against her pillow and seemed to weigh her options. Finally, she pushed herself up and out of bed.

"I'm awake anyway, so I may as well come," she said. "And the morning air is really good for the fur. Give me a few minutes and I'll meet you there."

"Great!" Paulina exclaimed happily. "We'll wait for you downstairs."

"Let's hope we see her soon," Paulina

WHISPERED to Violet as they headed out. "We know how long Coco's '**minute**' can be!"

Ten minutes later, the five friends were walking across the grounds of Mouseford Academy. The school was **calm** and ϙᴜⁱᵉ†, which happened a lot during the spring when some of the students went on weekend trips.

"It's so peaceful," Colette commented, looking around.

"Yes," Paulina agreed. "It's the perfect day to **PAINT** in nature."

"It really is," Nicky said thoughtfully. "I look forward to these creative workshops every spring."

The friends arrived in the garden to find a truly calm space. A few painting easels and stools were set up under a large oak tree. Nearby, there was a **GAZEBO** with a large table set for breakfast.

"Yum," Pam exclaimed as she hurried toward the buffet. "Look at all this **DELICIOUS** fruit and yogurt. What a way to start the day!"

Nicky and the others laughed. Some things would never change!

After they were done eating breakfast, Violet headed for one of the easels.

"We should get to work," she said happily. Then she placed a fresh canvas on the stand, opened her painting case, and carefully picked out the **PAINT TUBES** she would use for her work.

"You're so neat, Vi," Nicky commented admiringly as she watched her friend.

"Being organized helps me stay focused," Violet explained.

"Ah, that must be why my Paintings are always so chaotic!" Nicky replied, showing Violet her messy, half-finished canvas.

"If you want, I can help you work on a sketch first," Violet suggested.

"Really?!" Nicky exclaimed. "That would be amazing. Thank you!"

Nicky moved her easel closer to Violet's and smiled at her friend gratefully.

Paulina started working on a flowery bush while Pamela picked a large oak in the middle of the garden as the subject of her painting. Then the mouselets got to work, intent on painting and enjoying the sunny and peaceful day.

After they had been working for a while, Paulina's buzzing cell phone interrupted the silence.

She pulled her phone out of her pocket and gasped.

"What is it?" Colette asked her friend.

"I just got a text from Will Mystery!" Paulina exclaimed.

"Really?!" Nicky said, surprised.

"Yes!" Paulina said. "After the last time, I set up text forwarding from Thea's supersecret cell phone to my PHONE, in case of emergencies. The text is encrypted, but we can use a special software program to figure it out . . ."

"Well?" Violet asked impatiently, noticing the concerned look on Paulina's snout. "What does it say?"

"Not much, really," Paulina replied. "He said that we need to get to headquarters quickly because of an URGENT MATTER!"

Paulina held out the phone to show her friends.

"So Will Mystery wants us to head to the **Seven Roses Unit** right away," Colette

said thoughtfully. "I wonder why he didn't call like he usually does, though."

"It does seem strange that he would text us in the middle of the day without any explanation," Nicky agreed. "It must be an UNUSUAL case!"

"I'm sure he will explain everything when we get there," Paulina replied as she packed up her art supplies. "Let's go get ready. The helicopter will be here any minute!"

A NEW MISSION

The Thea Sisters kept thinking about Will's message as they headed back to their rooms. Will Mystery was the director of the **Seven Roses Unit**, a secret research center that studies hidden **FANTASY** worlds inhabited by creatures from fables and legends.

"I wonder which fantasy kingdom is in trouble this time," Pam said as she packed a small bag.

"Will didn't give us any details, so I'll just pack the essentials," Colette said, pulling out her enormouse three-piece **PINK** luggage set.

Pam couldn't help laughing at her friend.

"Okay, okay," Colette grumbled. "I'll just take a `small` backpack!"

Meanwhile, in the room next door, Nicky packed her own small bag.

"Compass, rope, flashlight, energy bars, **first aid kit** . . . done!" she said, satisfied with her work.

"Great," Paulina agreed as she zipped up her own backpack. "We don't have to bring too much with us now. Once we get there, Will will tell us what we'll need for our *mission*."

A few minutes later, the five mouselets met in the hallway.

"We'll need to be very careful," Paulina said softly as she looked out the window. It was almost noon, and the sun was high in the sky. It was an **ODD** time to leave for a mission: The Thea Sisters' trips to the Seven Roses Unit and to the different fantasy kingdoms had to remain **SECRET**! They had to get off campus without other students seeing them and wondering what they were up to.

The group left the building quietly, keeping a low profile. They scurried across Mouseford Academy's garden toward the North Lawn. Luckily the area was completely deserted because most students were either away for the weekend or in the cafeteria eating lunch.

The mouselets stared at the blue sky for a while, waiting.

There it is!

"*There it is!*" Colette suddenly shouted, pointing to a small dot in the distance. A few seconds later, the high-tech ultrasonic helicopter landed gently on the lawn, barely making a **sound**. The door opened.

"Quick!" Paulina exclaimed as she hopped inside. "Let's go!"

Her friends scurried aboard after her, and the door closed firmly behind them.

Violet looked out the window nervously. "Do you think anyone saw us?"

"I don't think so," Pam replied confidently.

The pilot welcomed them aboard and the helicopter took off. After a smooth, uneventful journey, the helicopter landed on a frosty iceberg. The pilot pushed a button and the ice cracked open, revealing a secret passageway that led through a tunnel to the **hidden** entrance to the Seven Roses Unit.

"Hang on!" Colette cried to her friends as the pilot maneuvered the craft down the dizzying passageway.

"Are you ready for a new adventure, mouselets?" Nicky asked as the helicopter touched down gracefully on the landing strip.

"I'm so curious to find out what this is all about!"

"Let's hope Will has some information to share with us," Violet said eagerly. "The more we know, the faster we can begin our MISSION!"

But the Thea Sisters were in for a surprise when they got off the helicopter.

WILL MYSTERY
wasn't there to meet them!

THE SEVEN ROSES UNIT

The headquarters of the Seven Roses Unit is hidden in the icy Arctic. Only the members of the unit know how to find the entrance.

THE ROSE PENDANT

Each researcher has a pendant that contains their personal information. It can be used as a key to open doors in the unit headquarters.

THE HALL OF THE SEVEN ROSES

In the heart of the unit is the Hall of the Seven Roses. It is a living map that shows every Fantasy World and reports on each one's condition. When a world is in danger, a crack appears in the map.

THE CRYSTAL ELEVATOR

A glass elevator is the gateway to the imaginary kingdoms. Only Will Mystery can operate the elevator using a special keyboard and a secret combination of musical notes. Then the power of music transports its occupants to a fantasy world!

AN UNEXPLAINED ABSENCE

The five friends looked around nervously.

"It's really odd that Will isn't here," Colette said. "He usually welcomes us when we arrive at the Seven Roses Unit."

"Maybe he's busy right now," Violet suggested.

"It isn't like him not to be here, though," Paulina pointed out. "Even the text he sent seemed as though it was written in a hurry."

"Something STRANGE is going on," Pam agreed.

The Thea Sisters headed straight to Will's office. They knocked on the door.

"Will?" Nicky called out. But there was no reply.

The five friends looked at one another,

unsure what to do next.

"Why don't we go to the *Hall of the Seven Roses*," Colette suggested. "If something is wrong in one of the fantasy kingdoms, I'm sure we'll find Will there."

"That's a good idea," Pam said, and she led the way. The mouselets knew that they would find a giant living map in the hall. If one of the fantasy worlds was in jeopardy, a crack would appear in the map to warn of the DANGER.

They scanned their rose-shaped CRYSTAL PENDANTS on the security scanner and entered the hall.

"Will, are you here?" Colette called out.

Her voice echoed in the empty room. Then

the mouselets' attention was drawn to the map.

"Oh no!" Pam exclaimed in alarm. "There are **cracks** everywhere!"

"These deep cracks go through all the fantasy worlds!" Nicky cried in disbelief.

"**Holey cheese**, I've never seen anything like this before," Paulina said, with a worried look on her snout. "The situation must be really bad!"

"We have to find Will," Colette said firmly.

The Thea Sisters searched throughout the entire Seven Roses Unit, but they couldn't find Will Mystery anywhere. It seemed the researcher had **VANISHED**! The five friends gathered again in the Hall of the Seven Roses, feeling disheartened.

"What do we do now?" Colette asked anxiously.

"Why don't we try Will's office?" Nicky

suggested. "He could have gone back there, and even if he hasn't maybe he's left us a *clue* that can help us figure out what's going on."

"But how will we get in if he hasn't shown up?" Violet asked. "The door is **locked**!"

"We can try using our CRYSTAL PENDANTS," Paulina offered. "After all, Will did ask us to come here today. What if he changed the **C O D E** to his office so that we could get in while he's away!"

"It's worth a try!" Violet said encouragingly.

Paulina was right: As soon as the Thea Sisters scanned their pendants, Will's office door opened.

They **HURRIED** inside and closed the door

behind them. Though they didn't squeak anything aloud, the Thea Sisters were all feeing **uneasy**. They had the feeling that Will's mysterious disappearance was just the first of a long list of **PROBLEMS** to solve!

PUZZLING CLUES

Once they were inside Will's office, Colette finally broke the silence.

"This is all very strange," she confessed. "Will asked us to come here right away, and yet he's **nowhere** to be found!"

"Something terrible must have happened," Violet said. "The cracks in the living map in the Hall of the Seven Roses confirm it."

"But Will must have left us some sort of CLUE or message to help us understand what's going on," Paulina said confidently as she looked through some files on the researcher's desk. "Yes! This is it!"

Paulina pointed to a card under a **GLASS** paperweight.

"It says Thea Sisters on it!" Nicky exclaimed happily.

Paulina picked up the note and began reading aloud.

Dear Thea Sisters,

I'm sorry I can't be here to meet you. I had to leave immediately for the fantasy kingdoms. The situation is critical, but I will explain everything when we meet. Bring the map that is in the second drawer and this paperweight; you will need them. I trust you. See you soon. —Will Mystery

"This note really doesn't explain much," Colette said as she picked up the red glass dome that had been sitting on top of the envelope.

"So far, this mission is full of mysteries with very few clues," Nicky remarked. Meanwhile, Violet was rummaging around in the second drawer of Will's desk.

5. AQUAMARINA

6. LAND OF FLOWERS

7. CRYSTAL KINGDOM

8. STARLIGHT KINGDOM

"Here's the **MAP**!" she exclaimed, showing it to her friends. "Will must have drawn this by paw."

"Holey cheese!" Pam exclaimed. "I can't make *SNOUT* or **TAILS** out of it."

"Will must have drawn this map after years of research and **trips** to the fantasy worlds," Nicky said. "Look, all the places we've visited are here: the Land of Erin, the Land of Minwa, the Land of Clouds, Aquamarina, the Land of Flowers, the Crystal Kingdom, and the Starlight Kingdom."

"And look!" Colette pointed out. "Here is one we have never been to . . . the Land of Colors!"

"There are question marks next to each of the kingdoms on here," Paulina observed. "I wonder what that means."

"I don't know," Violet said.

The friends looked at one another with worried expressions on their snouts. It felt like they had reached another **dead end**.

"Maybe we can do a computer search," Paulina proposed. "What do you think?"

Everyone agreed, so they headed to the **computer** room and scanned the map first, then the paperweight.

MAGICAL GATEWAY MAP

This map shows the gateways that connect the fantasy worlds. Every kingdom has two gateways. To reveal their locations, the user must solve a riddle. The map only works inside the fantasy kingdoms.

TIMEKEEPER STONE

This glass stone acts as a timekeeper: Its color changes to show how much time is left to complete the mission.

The Thea Sisters took a moment to process the information. Finally, Nicky spoke.

"Something tells me this will be our most difficult mission yet," she said.

"I think you're right," Violet agreed. "And we don't have a lot of *clues*! Right now, we have a magical map and a special stone."

"We also know something dangerous is threatening the kingdoms," Paulina continued.

"And it seems we have only a set amount of time to solve the problem," Colette concluded. "But how do we do that?"

"Since Will left us a map of the GATEWAYS between the different worlds, I'm guessing we'll have to travel from one kingdom to another," Paulina said.

"Right, but to do what?" Nicky asked in frustration. "I don't understand our mission!"

"Perhaps Will didn't really know himself,"

Violet speculated. "If he had known more, he would have told us."

"We don't even know where he is," Paulina said anxiously.

"Okay, let's stay calm," Colette said evenly. "The only thing we can do is follow the instructions he left in his note and be ready for anything.

Come on, mouselets, we can do this!"

So in spite of their many doubts, the Thea Sisters got ready to go to the fantasy kingdoms right away. They knew in their hearts that they were about to embark on the most *difficult* mission they had ever faced!

DESTINATION UNKNOWN

The Thea Sisters grabbed the map and the stone and headed down the long, winding corridor that led to the Crystal Elevator.

"This is the first time we'll travel to the **fantasy kingdoms** without Will," Paulina remarked nervously.

"That's true," Violet replied. "But we've done it many times before. Will must really TRUST us to assign us such an important task!"

"And we won't let him down, Sisters!" Pam exclaimed confidently.

A moment later, they arrived at the elevator with its golden trim and glimmering glass walls. This **MAGICAL** machine would transport them to the fantasy kingdoms.

"But where are we going, exactly?" Nicky asked.

"Good point, Nicky," Violet said. "There are **EIGHT** kingdoms on the map. Which one should we visit first?"

"Will didn't mention a specific destination in his note," Colette pointed out.

While the others were chatting, Paulina had scanned her **rose-shaped** crystal pendant, and the doors to the elevator had opened. She peered inside and found another clue.

"Sisters, **LOOK**!" Paulina exclaimed. "There's a note next to the keyboard. It's a sheet of music!"

"So, Will left us the destination after all," Violet said, smiling. "These **musical notes** will transport us there."

"Come on, then," Colette said eagerly. "Let's go!"

One by one, the mouselets stepped into the **MAGICAL** elevator. Violet began to play the **melody** on the keyboard and the doors slid closed. A second later, the elevator began to move.

Paulina smiled to herself. Will wasn't with them, but he had still been able to **HELP** them!

She looked down at the stone in her paws and hoped he was safe, wherever he was. She had to **trust** that everything would be all right.

"We have no idea where we're going, but it's no big deal," Pam said jokingly, trying to lighten the mood. "After all, there are only eight kingdoms, and we must be going to one of them!"

Everyone laughed and the tension broke.

"I think we're about to find out where." Paulina pointed out the window as the elevator began to slow.

When it finally came to a stop, the mouselets held their breath, waiting eagerly for the doors to open.

"Why, it's the Starlight Kingdom!" Pam cried when she saw the sparkling world of the fairies of the stars.

"This place is just as sparkly as I remember it!" Colette said happily.

"You're right, it looks exactly the same as the last time we were here," Paulina agreed. Then the Timekeeper Stone caught her eye. "Look! It's *changing color!*"

"We need to *HURRY*," Nicky said. "The countdown for our mission has just begun."

SOS AMONG
THE STARS

The Thea Sisters quietly observed the long
BRIDGES OF LIGHT that stretched across the sky.
They looked like golden tape connecting all
the planets in the *Starlight Kingdom*.

Finally, Violet squeaked, "Now what?"

"Well, we know the fantasy kingdoms are in
danger, but we have no idea what the threat
is," Paulina said.

"We should talk to our friends here in
Starlight," Violet suggested. "Maybe they can
HELP us figure out this mystery."

"Great idea," Colette agreed. "I'm sure
Astro and Cometta would be happy to tell
us what they know."

"Yes, but it takes a long time to get to
Brightstar Castle," Nicky pointed out.

"That's true," Paulina said slowly. Then she began to pace back and forth, thinking hard. Suddenly, she stopped, her snout lighting up. "I have an **idea**! I hope it works."

"What is it?" Violet asked

"Nicky, can you hand me the *flashlight*, please?" Paulina asked. "And I need something that will **REFLECT** the light. Colette, do you have a mirror?"

Her friend grinned. "Of course I do!" Colette replied. "You know I never leave home without one."

"I get it!" Nicky exclaimed suddenly. "You want to send a signal!"

Paulina nodded, smiling.

"I'll send a message in **MORSE CODE** using the flashlight," she explained. "The mirror will reflect the light. Coco, can you hold the mirror like this?"

Paulina showed her friend how to angle the mirror as she flashed the beam of light.

"What are you saying?" Pam asked.

"It's a simple request for help: **SOS**," Paulina replied. "That's three short flashes, three long flashes, and three more short flashes. I just hope someone sees it!"

She flashed the light over and over again, waiting patiently after each transmission. The Thea Sisters stared at the sky above them, hoping for a reply.

I hope someone sees it . . .

"If no one replies soon, we'll have to try something else," Violet said. "Time is ticking!"

"That's true," Nicky agreed.

All of a sudden, the mouselets saw a **BRIGHT LIGHT** appear on the horizon. It quickly moved closer and closer.

"Holey cheese!" Pam gasped. "It looks like . . ."

But before she could finish her sentence, a magnificent sparkling golden carriage appeared in the sky above. It was being pulled by two **BLUE DRAGONS**.

The Thea Sisters immediately recognized the two figures inside.

"It's Cometta and Prince Astro!" Nicky cried out, waving happily.

"Dear friends, welcome back!" the pair replied as the carriage landed in front of the Thea Sisters.

"Did you send an SOS signal?" Astro asked.

"Yes, we need your help," Paulina replied.

"Well, come aboard!" the prince said warmly, inviting them into the carriage. "What are you doing back in the *Starlight Kingdom*."

Prince Astro and Cometta **listened** closely as the Thea Sisters explained all that had happened so far.

"We haven't seen Will Mystery," Prince Astro replied.

"Oh," said Paulina, looking down in the snout. "We were hoping you had some news. I hope he's okay!"

"We'll find him," Colette said firmly. "But first we have to figure out what *exactly* is threatening the kingdoms."

"There is someone who can help," Cometta said **BRIGHTLY**. "Aphelia!"

"Aphelia is the wisest creature in the

Starlight Kingdom," Prince Astro agreed. "If anyone knows about the MYSTERIOUS threat to the fairy kingdoms, it's her!"

Cometta nodded. "And she may know what happened to Will Mystery," she added.

"Well, what are we waiting for?" Violet asked eagerly. "Let's go!"

Prince Astro pointed the dragons and the carriage toward the small planet that was home to Aphelia, the fairy who guarded the secrets of time.

Despite their worries, the Thea Sisters felt their hearts lift as they soared through the Starlight Kingdom's *enchanting* skies. All around them, an array of precious stars twinkled brightly as the dragons pulled the carriage through glowing light streams and past **colorful** planets toward Aphelia's home.

THE MAYHEM MIRROR

The dragons touched down gently, and the carriage came to a stop in a cloud of golden dust. As soon as the dust settled, Cometta, Prince Astro, and the Thea Sisters saw the elegant Aphelia standing before them. She was holding a bag full of mother-of-pearl sand.

"Prince Astro, Cometta, mouselets!" she exclaimed in surprise. "To what do I owe the pleasure of your UNEXPECTED visit?"

At first, no one squeaked.

"Oh no," Aphelia said, realization dawning on her. "From the looks on your snouts I can tell it's not good news. Please, come inside and **TELL ME** everything."

The group followed the fairy into her home, which was decorated with *hourglasses* of all shapes, sizes, and **colors**. She offered them some star anise tea and then gave them her full attention.

"I'm listening," she said with a gentle nod.

The Thea Sisters told her everything that had happened at the Seven Roses Unit, and they showed her the magical map and the Timekeeper Stone.

What happened?

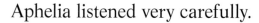
Aphelia listened very carefully.

"This is **SERIOUS**," the fairy said sadly.

"Can you help us, Aphelia?" Prince Astro asked. "Have you seen Will Mystery, or do you know where he might be?"

The fairy shook her head. "Unfortunately, I have not seen your friend," she replied. "But I think I have an idea as to what may be causing the threat to the kingdoms. If the Timekeeper Stone is active, it can mean only one thing: The Mayhem Mirror has been disturbed, and a terrible curse is about to be unleashed on the fantasy kingdoms!"

"What is the Mayhem Mirror?" Violet asked. It sounded awful.

"The Mayhem Mirror is an **ancient** object, created by a cruel witch a long time ago," the fairy explained. "Its power is terrifying: The mirror can release an icy-cold FOG OF FURY that can spread all over the kingdoms, enveloping everything from creatures to objects. The fog turns all that it touches to dust."

"Oh no!" Colette gasped. "How horrible."

"Yes, it is a truly wicked object," Aphelia confirmed. "The witch wanted to turn these beautiful kingdoms into dry **DESERTS**."

"I've never heard of this. Will didn't seem to be too worried about the kingdoms before," Paulina observed. "What changed?"

"That's true," Aphelia explained. "Years ago, the Grand Council of Fairies discovered the witch's plan and stopped her. The witch was forever banned from the kingdoms and the mirror was hidden in a secret place where no one would find it."

"Why wasn't the mirror **DESTROYED**?" Nicky asked, puzzled.

"It is impossible to destroy a **MAGICAL** object," Aphelia replied. "Instead it was buried by a knight in the farthest and most remote place in all the kingdoms: the Endless Void."

"That sounds like a terrifying place," Violet said, shivering.

"It is," Aphelia replied. "It is a huge gap that leads to nothing but **DARKNESS**. It is very dangerous to travel there, and fairy law forbids anyone from doing so."

You are banished forever!

"But someone must have done it and found the mirror," Pam pointed out. "And now all the fantasy kingdoms are in **danger**!"

"That's

right," the fairy replied. "The Fog of Fury will be released from the mirror when the time on the Timekeeper Stone runs out."

"We have to do something to stop this!" Colette exclaimed.

"Well, there is one antidote to the mirror's CURSE," Aphelia said.

"What is it?" the Thea Sisters asked hopefully.

"The power of the eight *Harmonies* can be unleashed to fight the fog," the fairy explained.

"Harmonies?" Nicky asked, perplexed. "But what are they?"

"Let me explain," Aphelia continued. "The face of the Mayhem Mirror is framed with eight **black pearls**; they hold the dark force that produces the fog."

"Yikes," Colette murmured. "It sounds like an extremely powerful curse."

Aphelia nodded. "It is," she said. "However, if the **eight pearls** are replaced with the *eight Harmonies* before the time runs out, the fog will be stopped, and the curse will be broken forever."

The Thea Sisters smiled. They finally understood their **MISSION**: find the eight Harmonies and save the eight kingdoms!

"Where do we find the eight Harmonies?" Violet asked the fairy.

"After they buried the mirror, the Grand Council of Fairies realized there was another way to protect the kingdoms," Aphelia went on. "Each kingdom has its own unique musical melody. The purest essence of each of these Harmonies can be found in just one teardrop from one of that kingdom's dragons.

"The magical power in each teardrop is so great it can protect each kingdom from evil.

Each kingdom's dragon tear is stored in a tiny sphere called a *Harmony*."

"Wow, these Harmonies must be very precious!" Colette exclaimed.

"They are," Aphelia agreed.

"How will we find them?" Nicky asked.

"A different guardian protects each Harmony," Aphelia continued. "You will need to find each guardian and ask for permission to collect it."

"We can use Will's map to navigate through the kingdoms!" Paulina said eagerly. "There are *eight kingdoms*, **eight teardrops**, and eight guardians . . ."

"We can't waste any time, Sisters," Pamela said quickly. "Aphelia, where can we find the guardian for the Starlight Kingdom?"

"Ah, yes," the fairy replied. "He lives on the First Star."

"We will take you, mouselets," Prince Astro offered.

"Thank you so much!" the Thea Sisters replied.

"And thank you, Aphelia," Cometta told the fairy. "We would have been lost without you."

"You are most welcome," the fairy replied. "I have one more piece of **advice**: In order to get each Harmony, you must show the guardians the Timekeeper Stone. It will be proof that you are on a special mission to protect the kingdoms."

"We'll remember," Violet agreed.

The mouselets smiled at the fairy and climbed back aboard the golden carriage with Prince Astro and Cometta. The next stop on their mission was Starlight Kingdom's **FIRST STAR**!

THE FIRST STAR

The flight to the First Star was very quiet. The Thea Sisters, Prince Astro, and Cometta were all thinking about what they had learned from Aphelia.

"Now I understand why Will left in such a **HURRY**," Paulina told her friends. "The threat of the Mayhem Mirror is the most **SERIOUS** one we've ever encountered!"

Then she noticed the concerned looks on Prince Astro's and Cometta's faces.

"Don't worry," she added. "We'll do everything we can to save the fantasy kingdoms, right, sisters?!"

"Of course!" her friends exclaimed.

"We'll never give up!" Colette added.

"Here we are," Prince Astro announced as the carriage approached a very special star.

It was carved out of the purest silver, and there were mysterious holes dotting the surface.

"It looks DESERTED," Nicky said.

"Don't be fooled by appearances," Prince Astro replied cryptically. "Aphelia is rarely wrong."

After the Thea Sisters had climbed down from the carriage, Cometta led them to one of the holes that had been cut in the star's bright surface.

"Why are we stopping here?" Nicky asked.

"This is where the guardian lives," Cometta replied, smiling.

"The guardian lives in there?" Violet asked as she peered into the hole. "But why?"

"This star is right at the crossroads of strong COSMIC STORMS," Cometta explained. "Sometimes the wind here is so strong that being outside is very dangerous.

Thankfully these storms are rare, but it's best to be prepared by living **underground**!"

"Hello!" the fairy called into the hole. "May we come in? It's Cometta."

A second later, a silver top hat popped out of the hole, followed by a smiling face. It was a leprechaun!

"Good morning, Cometta, Prince Astro," he greeted the fairies, then looked over at the

May we come in?

Thea Sisters. "To what do I owe the **honor** of your visit?"

"Good morning to you, too, Sigma," Prince Astro answered. "We are here with some friends who would like to ask you a question."

"May we come in?" Cometta repeated.

"Oh yes," the leprechaun replied. "Please do."

They followed him down a STEEP staircase that led deep underground.

The stairs led to a small room lit by CANDLES. The Thea Sisters followed the leprechaun through the first room and down some more into a second room. Sigma stopped there and gestured toward some colorful pillows on the floor, inviting his guests to make themselves comfortable.

Once they were all sitting, the prince cleared his throat.

"Dear Sigma, we know you have a very important **duty** in the Starlight Kingdom," he began. "These are the Thea Sisters. We are here to ask you to entrust them with Starlight's Harmony. They are on a very important mission, which they are undertaking for the good of all the kingdoms, including ours."

Sigma nodded, his face serious.

Prince Astro looked at Paulina, and she pulled the Timekeeper Stone from her pocket and showed it to the leprechaun.

"I see," Sigma replied gravely, scratching his chin. "I guess the situation really is serious. Follow me, please."

Sigma led them down another flight of stairs to a small room.

"This is where I keep the Harmony," he explained, gesturing to an empty glass case in the middle of the room.

"But where is it?" Colette gasped.

"I gave it to a Stranger who visited me just before you did," he replied.

"What do you mean?!" the prince asked.

"It's true, Your Highness," the leprechaun went on. "His name was Will Mystery."

"**WILL** was here?" Paulina exclaimed, relief flooding her voice.

"Yes, right before you got here," Sigma replied.

Yes, he had a stone, too!

"But Aphelia told us the Harmony can only be passed to someone who has the Timekeeper Stone," Paulina said.

She held out the stone again to Sigma, a confused look on her snout.

"Yes, that's right," Sigma replied. "He showed me the exact **S A M E** stone!"

The mouselets were CONFUSED. It seemed Will had been there with his own Timekeeper Stone, and he had taken the Starlight Kingdom's Harmony. What was going on?

"I wonder where he is now," Paulina said.

"Did he say which **way** he was going?" Violet asked.

"He didn't tell me directly, but I heard him whispering to himself," the leprechaun said.

"What was it?" Pam asked eagerly.

"He mumbled something about a **COLORFUL** sphere or marble," Sigma replied.

"But I don't know what he was talking about."

"If it's colorful, the object might be from the Land of Colors," Paulina said thoughtfully as they climbed the stairs. "That's next to the Starlight Kingdom on Will's map."

"Or it could be from the CRYSTAL KINGDOM, which is on the Starlight Kingdom's other side on the map!" Violet added uncertainly.

"There's no way to know for sure, is there?" Nicky said with a sigh.

Once they were aboveground, the mouselets thanked the leprechaun for his help.

"I hope you find what you are looking for," Sigma replied with a smile. "And GOOD LUCK with your mission, for all our sakes!"

"We'll do our best!" Paulina replied.

The Thea Sisters prepared to continue on their journey, determined and full of hope!

The Star of Stars
The Harmony of Generosity

Many years ago, a leprechaun lived in a dark galaxy bordering the Starlight Kingdom. Every day he would look out his window and admire the Star of Stars, the brightest celestial body in the Starlight Kingdom.

The leprechaun was tired of living in the dark, and he was enchanted by the star's pure light. So he embarked on a great journey across his own galaxy into the Starlight Kingdom. Once there, he intended to capture the Star of Stars and bring it back with him to his own dark galaxy.

The journey was long and arduous, but thanks to his determination and courage, the leprechaun finally reached his destination. The Star of Stars was shining brightly before him! The leprechaun felt like he was on top of the world. However, he was not aware of one important fact: The Star of Stars was the most fragile star in the entire kingdom.

As he moved close enough to the star to grab it, the precious orb of golden light began to break into pieces and fell into space.

The leprechaun was so frightened that he cried out loud. Two Star Fairies came to his aid immediately. Despite the fairies' best efforts, only two small pieces of the star could be saved. The leprechaun was sad. All he had wanted was to bring the precious gift of light to the creatures in his galaxy.

When they looked into his sad eyes, the fairies realized that the leprechaun had meant well, and they gave him one of the pieces they had rescued as a gift.

"For you!" they told the leprechaun. "May your galaxy never be dark again!"

The fairies kept the second piece and carved it into a star shape. This precious treasure was meant to remind all the creatures of the Starlight Kingdom of the great value of generosity.

THE FIRST RIDDLE

The Thea Sisters climbed into the carriage behind Prince Astro and Cometta. As soon as they were settled, Paulina pulled out the *Timekeeper Stone*.

"Look! It's changing color!" Colette observed. "I wonder what that means."

"I think it means we have to **HURRY**," Pamela replied urgently.

"But where are we going?" Paulina asked.

"Let's take a look at Will's map," Nicky suggested. She unfolded the parchment in front of her friends.

"Look, there are two **RIDDLES**," Violet pointed out. "There's one riddle for the Land of Colors and another for the Crystal Kingdom. Those are the lands that border the Starlight Kingdom on the map."

To go to the Land of Colors,
follow the brightest star.
Its rainbow-colored heart will
lead you near and far.

STARLIGHT KINGDOM

CRYSTAL KINGDOM

To go to the Crystal Kingdom, go
over the bridge of light.
Cross the desert dunes and the rope
of stars will lead you right.

"I have a feeling we have to first **decide** which direction to take and then SOLVe the corresponding riddle," Paulina said.

"Since Sigma mentioned a colorful sphere, I think it's the Land of Colors," Nicky said.

"But it could also be a colorful crystal carved into a sphere or marble," Colette pointed out uncertainly.

"Let's vote!" Violet suggested.

After a show of paws, the Crystal Kingdom won.

"Okay, now we need to solve the RIDDLE,"

Nicky said. "Where is this bridge of light?"

Prince Astro and Cometta overheard the mouselets chattering.

"Is there anything we can do to help?" Cometta asked kindly.

Nicky showed her the **MAP** with the riddles. Cometta studied it for a moment and then turned to speak quietly with Prince Astro.

"I think I know the bridge of light the riddle is talking about," Cometta said.

"**Perfect!**" Nicky replied. "Let's go!"

The fairies led the Thea Sisters a short distance and Prince Astro pointed to the dazzling golden ribbon that crossed the sky.

"I'm not sure about the rest of the riddle, though," Cometta said. "The desert and the rope of stars could be anywhere."

"We'll figure it out," Colette said confidently.

"And we will head back to update the Grand

Council of Fairies immediately," Prince Astro told them.

"Thank you so much!" Violet said.

"Good luck!" Cometta replied with a smile. "We know you can do it, mouselets!"

"We won't let you down," Colette reassured them as she and the other Thea Sisters bid the fairies farewell.

"Please be careful!" Cometta called back to them as the golden carriage soared off into the sky.

On their own again, the five friends stepped toward the sparkling bridge of light that connected one planet to the next like a strip of golden tape. They began to walk across, and soon they saw a star with a surface covered in what looked like hills of gold sand.

"Holey cheese!" Pam exclaimed. "Those must be the desert dunes!"

"Great!" Violet exclaimed happily. "We're getting closer."

"Right, but how will we find a rope of stars here?" Nicky asked hopelessly.

"Let's try to just take some deep breaths and focus," Colette said reasonably.

"The rope is probably buried in the sand,"

Look at those sand dunes!

Come on, let's go!

Pamela suggested. "I can't see where else it would be hidden."

The Thea Sisters began to explore the sand dunes, carefully looking for **CLUES**.

Suddenly, something sparkly caught the corner of Paulina's eye.

"Look over here, girls!" she exclaimed.

The Thea Sisters hurried over to where Paulina was standing. They looked down at the ground and saw a GLIMMER of light shining through the grains of sand.

Colette knelt down and picked up a pawful of the golden sand. It felt as **soft** and **warm** as silk. Then, suddenly, she felt something firm in the sand. With a tug, she pulled up a shimmering golden rope.

"You found it!" Violet cried. "It's the rope of stars."

Let's dig it up!

"Well done, Colette!" Paulina **EXCLAIMED** happily.

The five friends gently and carefully pulled the rope up.

"Be careful," Paulina warned them. "It's very

delicate, and we don't want it to break!"

Finally, the last grain of sand slid off the rope, and it was completely free.

"Grab the rope, everyone," Colette said. "Let's go!"

The Thea Sisters followed the rope, CLIMBING one dune after the next. Each one was deeper and taller than the last. When they had finally reached the tallest peak, a very strong WIND started blowing.

"Close your eyes to keep the sand out!" Nicky cried. "Hold on TIGHT and don't let go of the rope for any reason!"

The mouselets squeezed their eyes shut, and a few moments later, the dust had settled.

THE NIGHT
GEMS PATH

When the sandstorm had stopped, the Thea Sisters opened their eyes and looked around. They were no longer in the Starlight Kingdom. Instead, they found themselves in the middle of a **DARK** **TUNNEL**.

"We made it!" Pamela said in relief. "We're through the magic gateway."

"Right, but where are we?" Violet asked, frowning.

Colette pointed ahead of them. "Look, I can see a light up there," she said.

The mouselets walked toward it. As they got closer, the light shone **redder** and **redder** until Nicky, who was the first in line, stopped.

Pamela and Violet bumped into her, and behind them Paulina and Colette stopped suddenly, too.

Stop!

"**WHAT IS IT?**" Colette asked. "Why did you stop?"

Nicky moved aside so her friends could take a look for themselves.

"**HOLEY CHEESE!**" Pam exclaimed.

The five mouselets were standing at the edge of a rocky cliff overlooking a large pool of bubbling hot lava! Rising FLAMES and scorching steam rose all around them.

Just then, Colette had a realization.

"I know where we are!" she cried in surprise.

"Where?" Nicky asked.

"We're in the Crystal Kingdom, in the **DARK CAVES**!" Colette continued.

"Oh no!" Violet said. "How did we end up here?"

"I don't know," Pamela replied, shaking her head. "What do we do now?"

"We have to go back," Paulina replied. "It won't be easy to follow the maze of tunnels through the cave, but I think it's the only way out!"

She pulled out the Timekeeper Stone from her pocket.

"Look!" Nicky exclaimed. "It keeps changing **COLOR**."

"I know," Paulina said, studying the stone closely. Then she held it out to her friends. "There's something else happening, too."

It's showing us the way!

"What is it?" Violet asked, curious.

"The center of the stone **glows** more or less brightly depending on which direction we turn."

"Do you mean the stone is telling us something?" Pamela asked.

"Maybe," Paulina said. "I think we should go this way to get to the exit."

"It would be amazing if this stone worked like a **compass**, too," Colette said.

"There's only one way to find out," Pam said. "Let's go!"

The sisters walked along a series of dark, narrow tunnels, using the glowing stone as their guide. When it glowed brighter, they would make a turn. Finally, they reached the exit.

"We made it!" Nicky rejoiced, taking a deep breath of fresh air.

"We did, but where are we now?" Violet wondered, looking around.

The mouselets were in the middle of a dark plateau. All around them they could see nothing but rocky **desert**. There was no vegetation in sight.

"What a **barren** place," Colette remarked.

"Doesn't it seem familiar?" Paulina asked her friends as she continued to lead them with the glowing stone.

"Yes, it does," Violet agreed. "I feel like I've been here before . . ."

The Night Gems Path!

It's open!

Suddenly, the ground began to slope UPWARD and the mouselets found themselves going over a hill.

At the top, they came to a place they knew very well.

"Of course!" Pam exclaimed. They were standing in front of a gigantic gate. "This is the beginning of the Night Gems Path!"

"You're right," Nicky exclaimed in surprise. "We walked through this gate on our last mission in the Crystal Kingdom."

"But we don't have the KEY this time," Paulina said, her snout serious.

"Look!" Violet squeaked happily as they got closer. "The gate is open!"

"Great!" Pam exclaimed. "Let's go!"

And without another word, the mouselets walked confidently through the gate toward the magical Night Gems Path!

IN BERYL'S CHAMBERS

The Thea Sisters walked along the Night Gems Path, their eyes wide. The path had *changed* since their last visit! What had once been an underground garden full of colorful flowers was now a tunnel lined in thousands of flower-hued **GEMS**. They were embedded in the walls and ceiling of the tunnel, forming elaborate geometric shapes.

"It's almost like we are walking inside a sparkly TREASURE CHEST!" Violet exclaimed.

"It is," Paulina agreed in amazement. Then she looked down at the Timekeeper Stone. It had started to glow again. "Mouselets, stop! I think there's something here!"

"I can't see anything," Pam argued. "It's just a solid wall . . ."

Paulina and Colette stopped to carefully study the tunnel's gem-and-crystal-covered surface.

"There's a repeating PATTERN in the decoration," Paulina noticed aloud. "Can you see it? It looks like . . ."

". . . a **door**!" Colette exclaimed. "It's almost completely hidden by the CRYSTALS."

It looks like . . .

. . . a door!

"That stone in the middle might be a **handle**," Paulina pointed out. She grabbed the gem and turned, and the door squeaked and opened up to reveal a **SECRET CAVE** completely covered in sparkling red stones. A small fairy was standing in the middle of the room.

"Holey cheese, it feels like we're standing inside a ruby!" Pam exclaimed.

"**INCREDIBLE!**" Colette gasped in wonder.

"Welcome," the fairy greeted them warmly. "My name is Beryl."

"We are the Thea Sisters," Colette replied. "We are looking for the Crystal Kingdom's Harmony. Can you tell us where we can find the Harmony's guardian?"

The fairy frowned and looked at the mouselets **suspiciously**.

"I am the guardian," she said. "But I cannot just hand over the Harmony to anyone who asks."

Paulina showed the fairy the *Timekeeper Stone*. Its color changed from red to orange.

The fairy's eyes grew wide.

"You have the Timekeeper Stone?" she asked in surprise. "This means you are the chosen ones! In that case, I will give you the Harmony. But first you must promise me you will be extremely careful. It is fragile and very precious."

"Of course!" the mouselets exclaimed. "We will protect the Harmony!"

The fairy put on a pair of silver gloves and gently removed a transparent sphere from a large glass case.

"If this Harmony is still here, maybe Will went to the Land of Colors," Colette whispered to Paulina.

"That means we're going in the opposite direction," Paulina said with a sad sigh.

"Perhaps it's better that way," Colette pointed out. "By going in separate directions, we cover more ground and collect the Harmonies faster."

The fairy showed the sphere to the mouselets before she slipped it into a velvet pouch and passed it to Violet. A shiny crystal butterfly the color of **sapphires** was encased in the sphere.

"The butterfly looks like it is moving," Colette observed.

"The Harmonies are not simple objects," Beryl explained. "Each one contains the purest essence of each fantasy kingdom. Protect the Crystal Kingdom's Harmony and keep it safe always! The dragon's tear inside

Beryl

is precious, and the sphere is fragile."

"Is that why you wore those silver gloves when you handled it?" Nicky asked.

"Yes," the fairy replied, nodding solemnly. "Dragon **TEARS** are very sensitive to a fairy's touch."

"Thank you, Beryl," Pamela said.

"We promise we will take good care of the Harmony," Violet added reassuringly.

The fairy smiled and walked the Thea Sisters to the exit, where she wished them good luck and bade them farewell. The **door** closed softly behind them.

"What now?" Violet asked her friends.

"The map!" Nicky exclaimed. "Let's look at the next riddle and decide which way to go."

The Sapphire Butterfly

The Harmony of Hope

A long time ago, a fairy lived in the Crystal Kingdom. Her name was Joy, and everyone knew her for her happy and beautiful smile. Each morning, Joy would smile at the world around her, and she would sing and fly happily through the kingdom.

However, one day something strange happened. Joy was out for a walk in the forest behind her home. There, she saw a pretty butterfly fluttering through the trees. Suddenly, Joy came upon a witch. The butterfly danced happily around the witch's head, annoying her. The witch tried to cast a spell on the butterfly, but her spell missed. The witch raised her wand to strike again, and Joy flew in front of the butterfly in an attempt to stop the witch.

This time the spell worked, and it struck both Joy and the tiny insect. Joy's wings froze instantly, and the pretty butterfly turned to stone. The fairy held the stone creature in her hands and cried for a long time.

Joy wandered the forest desperately for days, until one night when there was a full moon. She looked up at the glowing moon and had the sudden realization that she had to fight the spell. She would learn to fly again, no matter how long it took!

Every morning, Joy tried to fly again, her strength and determination growing each day. She held the little stone butterfly in her hands every time. Finally, one morning, Joy flapped her wings, and flew again.

"I did it!" the little fairy exclaimed happily. "I'm flying!"

When Joy opened her hands, the fairy realized that the stone insect had come to life again as a beautiful sapphire butterfly, as bright as the fairy's newfound happiness!

THE JADE JUNGLE

The Thea Sisters found themselves on the Night Gems Path again. The secret door that led to Beryl's chamber had *disappeared*, blending in with the tunnel's sparkling crystal walls.

"The door is gone," Violet noticed.

"Look!" Paulina exclaimed as she held out the Timekeeper Stone. "The stone isn't **glowing** anymore, either!"

"Perhaps it's because we have the Harmony now and don't need to get inside," Colette guessed.

Violet shook her head. "These gateways between the kingdoms are really **DIFFICULT** to find!" she said. "Without the riddles from Will, we would be lost!"

"You said it, Sister!" Nicky agreed. "And squeaking of riddles, here's the next one."

She pulled out the map from her backpack.
Her friends gathered around her, studying
the parchment. They **focused** on the riddle that
would lead them to the Land of Flowers, their
next destination. Nicky read aloud:

To get to the Land of Flowers,
find the glowing jade.
Have trust in yourselves, then
jump the archway before it fades.

CRYSTAL KINGDOM

LAND OF FLOWERS

"The JADE JUNGLE!" the five mouselets
exclaimed.

"I'm sure that's what the first part of the
riddle means," Pam said. "I'm not so sure
about the second part of the riddle, though."

"Let's get to the Jade Jungle first," Colette

suggested. "Once we get there, we can ask the **Jade Fairies** for their help. They were so nice to us the last time we were there."

"Great idea, Coco," Paulina agreed. "Come on, let's go!"

The mouselets started off right away, walking fast. They wanted to get to the Jade Jungle quickly. As they walked, the Timekeeper Stone kept changing color: It was now a deep yellow . . .

When they got to the jungle, the five friends were as mesmerized as they had been the first time they visited the Crystal Kingdom.

The trees looked like sculptures covered in glowing green leaves.

"We're here!" Violet exclaimed,

looking all around her.

"The riddle mentioned an archway," Colette said. "What do you think that means?"

But before anyone could answer, the road they were walking on was blocked by a river.

"Now what?" Paulina asked in dismay.

"The tide is too strong for us to walk or swim across," Nicky said. "We'll have to walk along the river until we find a bridge."

"A **bridge**!" Paulina exclaimed. "You're a genius, Nicky!"

"What did I say?" Nicky replied, confused.

"The riddle!" Paulina explained. "The archway we're looking for might actually be a bridge that **arches** over the river! Come on, let's go!"

The five mouselets walked carefully along the river, weaving among the jade trees. Finally, they came upon a small wooden bridge.

"I remember this place!" Violet remarked. "This is the entrance to Fang's territory."

Fang was a beautiful white wolf who served as a GUARDIAN of the jungle and its creatures.

"Do you think that by walking across the bridge we will also walk through the magic gateway?" Colette wondered aloud, unsure.

"We won't know until we try," Pam replied.

But before they could take a step, a sound interrupted them.

"What you are looking for is not here," came a deep, rumbling voice.

The Thea Sisters turned to see a proud white wolf emerge from behind a bush. The mouselets recognized him right away: It was **FANG**!

Even though the animal looked scary, Violet stayed strong.

Fang

"Brave Fang, do you remember us?" she asked. "We are the Thea Sisters. We've come back to the Crystal Kingdom because we are searching for the eight Harmonies. We need your **HELP** for the sake of the Crystal Kingdom and all the other kingdoms as well. Do you know where we can find the passageway to the Land of Flowers?"

The wolf stared at the mouselet with his BRIGHT eyes for a long time. Finally, he spoke.

"I remember you mouselets," he said, nodding. "Follow me."

The Thea Sisters followed the wolf into the thick jungle until they reached the outskirts of the Jade Fairies' village. In front of them, a wooden bridge over the river led to a village surrounded by mountains.

The mouselets thanked Fang for his help, and the wolf nodded good-bye. Across the river, fairies looked at the newcomers **curiously** from the windows of their tiny homes.

Nicky took the lead, walking ahead. But before she stepped onto the bridge, she turned around and reached out for her friends' paws. The riddle said they had to take a **LEAP OF FAITH**, and there was no one in the world Nicky trusted more than her friends.

Holding paws firmly, the **THEA SISTERS**

walked confidently across the bridge. When they were one pawstep away from the other side, they held their breath and closed their eyes. Then they took the final step together.

For a moment, it felt like they were floating. But just a few seconds later, their paws landed on the ground once again. The mouselets opened their eyes to find they had indeed **crossed** the gateway into a new kingdom. They were in the middle of an endless *fragrant* field of flowers!

TRAPPED BY THE ORCHIDS

Violet stared out at the beautiful fields before her. "How incredible!" she breathed, awestruck.

"What a sweet SMELL!" Colette said as she took a few steps toward the gorgeous blooms.

"I wonder what these are called," Nicky said. "They look like some kind of orchid."

"Yes, but they have an UNUSUAL shape," Pam remarked. "They almost remind me of seashells!"

Pam took a step closer to one of the flowers, and it suddenly bent its stem forward and grabbed her leg firmly between its petals.

"Holey cheese!" Pam cried out. "Let me go!"

But the plant kept its grip.

"Pam, I think it's a CARNIVOROUS PLANT!" Nicky shouted.

"What?" Pam replied, a look of fear on her snout. "Get me out of here!"

She tried to wriggle free, but the plant wouldn't let go. The other mouselets gathered around their friend to help, but they didn't know what to do. The flower held tightly to Pam's leg.

"Let go of me right now!" Pam ordered the plant. But the green jaws wouldn't budge.

Suddenly, Violet cried out.

We'll help you!

Let me go!

"Mouselets!" she shouted. "One of them got me, too!"

"And me!" Paulina added as green tendrils twisted around her legs, holding her in place.

Out of the corner of her eye, Colette noticed a plant reaching toward her.

"Don't even **THINK** about it!" Colette told the plant fiercely. But the giant flower stretched out two leaves and grabbed her elbows.

"I had no idea there were **CARNIVOROUS** plants in the Land of Flowers!" Nicky cried out as she jumped away from the plants to safety. "Hang on, girls, I'll **rescue you**!"

Nicky heard a voice behind her.

"What's going on here?" asked a deep, firm voice.

When the mouselet turned around, she saw a face she knew well.

"**PRINCE HELIOS!**" Nicky exclaimed, surprised.

"Nicky?" he replied in equal surprise.

"Yes, it is," Nicky said quickly. "Please, we need your help! These **CARNIVOROUS** plants have trapped my friends and I don't know what to do."

"Don't worry, we'll take care of it," the prince reassured her. Then he turned to the entourage of knights standing beside him. "My dear **Knights of the Sunflower**, please free these mouselets!"

Upon hearing the command, the knights prepared to attack.

"No, wait!" Nicky cried. "Please don't hurt the plants!"

"We are not going to harm

Prince Helios

them in any way. Don't worry," Helios replied with a reassuring smile.

The mouselets watched in amazement as the knights crossed the tips of their MAGIC SWORDS to form the shape of a star over the plant that was holding Colette's arms tight.

A moment later, the large leaves released their hold on the mouselet. Once Colette was free, it was Pam's turn, then Violet's, and finally Paulina's.

"Is everyone all right?" Prince Helios asked.

"We are now," Paulina replied.

The prince smiled. "You weren't in **DANGER**," he said. "They weren't going to hurt you."

"What do you mean?" Violet asked doubtfully. "Aren't they carnivorous?"

Prince Helios shook his head. "They are Caressing Orchids. They feed on flying flowers, not mice."

"What are flying flowers?" Colette asked, curious.

"They are special flowers that grow on some tree trunks," one of the knights explained. "Usually they fall off and scatter in the air, where they look like delicate butterflies."

"Here they are," said another knight, pointing at the sky.

Nicky exclaimed in wonder.

A moment later, one of the orchids caught two flying flowers and closed its leaves around them tightly.

"If the orchids weren't going to eat us, why did they attack?" Pam asked Prince Helios, a confused look on her snout.

"They weren't attacking you," he replied, chuckling. "They were just playing and joking around!"

"Well, it wasn't very fUNNY!" Colette said as she straightened her fur and her clothes.

"Yes, I can see how scary it must have been for you," another blond knight said. "But what's important is that everyone is okay now."

"OH YES!" Colette said. "We're fine now . . . thanks to all of you!"

"What has brought you back to our kingdom?" Prince Helios asked.

"We are on a mission to find the Harmony from the Land of Flowers," Colette explained. "We have to stop the FOG OF FURY from being released over all the fantasy kingdoms!"

Prince Helios's face darkened. "I have heard the story of the Mayhem Mirror," he said. "But I thought the threat was gone **forever**!"

"I'm afraid someone stole the mirror from its hiding place in the ENDLESS

VOID," Paulina explained, a sad look on her snout. "The mirror has since unleashed the evil **CURSE** of the black pearls across the kingdoms."

"Are you telling me that all the kingdoms are in danger and could be destroyed at any time?" Prince Helios asked.

The THEA SISTERS were silent for a moment. Then Pamela spoke.

"Unfortunately, yes," she said. "But we are on a **mission** to stop the fog, and we won't give up!"

"I understand," Prince Helios replied gravely. "Get on our unicorns, mouselets. We will take you to the Fairy of Good Counsel. She will let you know where you can find the guardian of the Land of Flowers' Harmony."

THE SECRET OF THE EMERALD GEM

The Thea Sisters climbed onto the majestic unicorns and flew through the amazing Land of Flowers countryside. They rode by the home of the Perfume Fairies, distillers of the most fragrant scents. Then they crossed the Green Petal Plain, where they greeted the Dewdrop fairies, who were busy sprinkling dew on the field's blossoms. Finally, they landed in a familiar place.

"This is the Hawthorn Labyrinth, home of the Fairy of Good Counsel!" Prince Helios said.

"Look!" Paulina said. She held out the stone. "It's **FLASHING** again."

"I wonder if that means the Fairy of Good Counsel is the Harmony's guardian," Pamela said thoughtfully.

"We'll **FIND OUT** soon enough," Nicky replied.

After taking them to the entrance of the maze, Helios and his knights said good-bye.

"We must return to the Golden Dahlia Palace to inform Princess Flora and Princess Farrah about the threat to our kingdom," he explained. "We have complete **FAITH** in you, mouselets."

"Of course you must go!" Colette said. "Thank you for everything, Prince Helios."

The knights climbed on their unicorns and took off. When the Thea Sisters could no longer see the winged creatures in the sky, they gathered their courage and stepped carefully into the labyrinth. The bushes immediately began to shift, blocking their way.

"Holey cheese!" Pam exclaimed.

"Do you remember how it worked the last time we were here with Princess Flora?" Violet asked.

"Yes!" Colette cried suddenly. "There are no wrong turns or dead ends in the Hawthorn Labyrinth."

"That's right," Nicky continued. "We have to have **FAITH** and TRUST the labyrinth to guide us safely to its center."

"How can we be sure that's still true?" Paulina wondered aloud. "If the Harmony is here, maybe the labyrinth is behaving differently in order to protect it!"

The passageway is narrowing!

What should we do?

"You could be right," Pam said. "This passageway isn't blocked, but it keeps getting narrower!"

"What if it's a TRICK to test us?" Paulina said anxiously.

"If it is, then we will prove ourselves worthy," Violet said confidently. "We've made our way through this maze before. If we just have faith, I know we can do it again!"

"Well said, Sister!" the others agreed.

"Let's go!" Paulina said bravely.

She walked ahead of the others. The branches extended out, but they didn't touch her. Instead, some soft blossoms fell on her fur. Paulina continued on, the other mouselets right behind her. At one point, it looked as though Paulina had **disappeared** into the bushes.

Then the hawthorn branches quietly pulled back, making way for the others to follow her.

Finally, the Thea Sisters arrived at the home

of the Fairy of Good Counsel, which was at the center of the maze.

"*Is someone here?*" a gentle voice asked from inside the little house. A moment later, the fairy appeared holding a basket of flowers. She did not seem surprised to see the Thea Sisters.

"You are here, then," she said simply.

"Were you expecting us?" Violet asked.

"The hawthorn was restless today: I could hear the branches shifting in the breeze," the fairy explained. "It acts like that when it senses danger. Please, **come inside**."

"Thank you," the mouselets replied, following the fairy into her home.

The fairy welcomed them into her living room and offered them a fruit drink.

"We are here on an **IMPORTANT** mission," Colette explained as she sipped her juice. "We have come for the Land of Flowers' Harmony."

"You are the guardian, right?" Pam asked.

The fairy nodded.

"We have the **Timekeeper Stone**," Paulina said, holding out the glowing orb. It was flashing a deep **YELLOW**, like a little sun.

The fairy studied the stone carefully.

You are here ...

The Fairy of Good Counsel

"You still have some time left to **collect** all the Harmonies," she told them. "But you will need to move quickly."

"How do you know how much time we have left?" Violet asked, curious.

"The stone changes **COLORS** like a **RAINBOW**," the fairy explained. "When you began, it was red, then orange, then yellow. When you've reached the end of the rainbow and the stone is completely black, the Fog of Fury will be released."

"That means we've used up half the TIME we have available," Violet said.

The fairy nodded. "Now it's time to go," she said swiftly. "The Harmony is not here."

"What do you mean?" Pam asked, confused. "Isn't it your duty to protect it?"

"Yes," the fairy replied. "That's why I am storing it in the Emerald Gem. Please, follow me."

"What is the Emerald Gem?" Nicky asked as she and the other Thea Sisters walked alongside the fairy.

"Be patient, my dear," the fairy answered. "You will soon see it with your own eyes . . ."

Once they reached the back of the house, the fairy stopped.

She pulled out a LITTLE CRYSTAL VIAL hanging from a necklace around her neck. Then she removed a dropper from the vial.

"Take a step back, please," she instructed as she released three drops of a sparkling liquid onto the grass in front of her. The earth shook, and a moment later a large **emerald-green** gem emerged.

"Here it is!" the fairy exclaimed. "It's the best hiding place for precious objects."

Then she began to sing sweetly and softly in an unknown language. Slowly, the mysterious gem opened up and the Thea Sisters saw a transparent sphere at its center.

"Holey cheese!" Pamela said in awe. "It's the *Harmony*!"

The fairy pulled on a pair of gloves similar to the ones Beryl had worn. Then she gently lifted the sphere out of the gem.

The Flower of the Wind

The Harmony of Trust

The Land of Flowers wasn't always lush and full of fragrant flowers and green fields. A long time ago, part of this kingdom was bare and desolate, just like a desert. No matter how hard the creatures in the Land of Flowers worked to grow something there, not even the tiniest plant flourished.

One day, a Perfume Fairy known for her excellent sense of smell sniffed an unfamiliar scent. It was a fragrance that hadn't come from her own garden, so she knew it had to have been blown that way by the wind.

Curious, she decided to investigate. She followed the smell, and after a long journey, she ended up in the desert. The landscape around her was completely desolate and dry except for a single, beautiful blue flower.

The fairy realized immediately that it had been the source of the smell.

"What an amazing flower!" she gasped in delight. "This flower is special: It contains every fragrance in the kingdom!"

At that moment, a gust of wind blew and one flower petal dropped from the beautiful blue blossom. The fairy picked it up and gently placed it in one of the cracks in the dry, barren land. A moment later, a new flower sprouted exactly where she had placed the petal!

Another gust of wind came, and more petals fell from the blue blossom. New flowers sprouted up quickly wherever the petals landed. When the blossoms covered the entire desert, the fairy pulled one for herself. She would guard it forever as a precious treasure and as a symbol of strength!

"Please take good care of it," she said, handing the sphere to Colette.

"Of course!" Colette whispered softly.

"Now go," the Fairy of Good Counsel urged them. "You have an important mission to accomplish."

The Thea Sisters **THANKED HER** and retraced their steps through the labyrinth. As they walked through the Hawthorn Labyrinth, they thought about the *wonders* they had seen so far on this *journey* through the fantasy kingdoms. They knew now more than ever how important it was for them to complete their mission successfully!

ROSY SNOWDROP VALLEY

Paulina carried the Timekeeper Stone as they walked. It was still glowing a bright yellow, but the edges were starting to turn a pale green.

"I'm so glad we know for sure why the stone changes color now," Violet said.

"Yes, I know!" Paulina said happily. "It was red when we began, then orange, and now it's yellow."

"It still has to turn green, then **blue**, then indigo, and finally **violet**," Nicky added.

"And if it gets to black, then the Fog of Fury will be released," Colette concluded.

"I'm a little worried," Violet said. "We've only been able to collect two Harmonies so far."

"Let's not lose faith, mouselets!" Nicky said. "Two Harmonies are more than we had when we started."

Then she took Will's map and read the new RIDDLE aloud.

To go to Aquamarina, first find the pink blossoms in snow. Next, climb up the hillside, and on to the next kingdom you'll go.

LAND OF FLOWERS

AQUAMARINA

The next stop was clearly Aquamarina, the enchanting Land of the Sea. As soon as Nicky finished reading, the mouselets began trying to solve the riddle.

"Maybe we should be looking for snowdrop flowers," Violet suggested.

"But snowdrops are white, not pink," Colette pointed out.

"Hmmm, good point, Colette," Paulina said. "Then again, nothing in the fantasy kingdoms is ever quite what it seems, is it? I think we should start by looking for a **snowy** hillside."

The others agreed. They began climbing the nearest hill in the hopes that they might see a snow-covered mountain from its top.

But as they climbed, Violet was distracted by a *BUZZING* sound in her ear.

"Do you hear that?" she asked her friends.

"Yes," Paulina replied, nodding. "It's a buzzing sound, and it's getting louder."

Violet looked up and saw a swarm of bees approaching them.

"Bees!" she cried. "They're flying this way!"

The mouselets continued up the hill, moving as quickly as they could.

"They're following us!" Colette said anxiously as the **insects** hovered above them.

"Do you think they want the Harmony?" Pam asked, worried.

"Don't worry," Nicky replied reassuringly. "They won't be able to get it. I put it in my backpack!"

"Wait a minute," Paulina said suddenly. She had gotten a closer look at the bees, and she **recognized** them right away. "Those aren't bees . . . they're **Bee Fairies** from Honeyville!"

"Who are you?" one of the Bee Fairies asked. "And what are you doing here?"

"We are the Thea Sisters," Colette replied. "We've been to Honeyville before and we know Queen Melania, the Queen Bee Fairy."

"We helped the Flower Fairies when the roses in the Timeless Rose Garden were in

DANGER," Paulina explained.

"Is it really you?!" the fairy asked. "I was far away on a mission when that happened, but I know the story."

"We are back because there is a new **THREAT** to the Land of Flowers and all the fantasy kingdoms," Colette went on.

"My friends and I will be happy to help you with your mission," the fairy said.

"We are looking for a snowy hillside with blooming pink flowers. Do you know it?" Nicky asked quickly.

"Of course!" the fairy replied, smiling proudly. "You mean the Rosy Snowdrop Valley! We can take you there!"

We are the Thea Sisters!

Oooh!

The Thea Sisters followed the Bee Fairies on what seemed like a NEVER-ENDING journey. Finally, they reached a valley that had been dusted with snow. Its hillsides were dotted with very tall stems with enormouse pink flowers on them: These were the unusual rosy snowdrops the riddle mentioned!

The Thea Sisters thanked the Bee Fairies for their help and waved good-bye to the tiny buzzing creatures.

Then they turned their attention back to the map's RIDDLE.

They began climbing slowly up the hillside.

Once they reached the top, the mouselets realized that the snowdrops had changed shape! The center of each flower had widened, and the petals had multiplied. The blossoms began to drop off the stems, landing in the CRYSTAL-CLEAR water of the icy lake below. Each flower now looked like a tiny pink boat.

"Incredible!" Nicky whispered. Without even realizing it, the Thea Sisters had crossed the magic door to the

KINGDOM OF AQUAMARINA!

The flowers have changed ..

AN UNDERWATER ADVENTURE

The Thea Sisters found themselves once again swimming among **multicolored** fish through water plants that swayed here and there with the tide. The light that trickled down from the surface made the water all around them sparkle magically.

"I can't believe it!" Paulina said happily. "We're in Aquamarina again!"

"We went from the **sky** to the **OCEAN**, all in the same day!" Colette said in awe.

"How fantastic!" Violet said softly as she took in her surroundings. She and her friends swam for a while until they noticed an underwater current that was making small **WAVES** on the surface of the water. It looked like a river under the ocean.

"Isn't that the *DIAMOND CURRENT*?" Violet asked.

"I think so!" Pamela agreed.

"If I remember correctly, following the current will take us directly to Queen Anemone's PINK PEARL CASTLE," Colette reminded them.

Paulina looked down at the Timekeeper Stone in her paws.

"The stone and the current point in the same direction!" she announced.

"Then we know exactly what to do," Nicky said. "Follow that current!"

The Thea Sisters swam confidently into the **FLOWING** stream of water, sure that they would soon arrive at the castle. After swimming for some time, though, their surroundings seemed the same.

Colette turned to Paulina.

"Has the stone changed at all?" she asked.

"Do you think we're getting any closer?"

Before she could respond, Paulina looked down to see an enormouse pink **jellyfish** bobbing just below them, partly hidden in shadow.

"Holey cheese!" Pam cried as she spotted the creature.

"Let's not panic," Nicky said reasonably, trying to reassure her friends.

"Nicky's right," Paulina said. "It's only a **jellyfish** . . ."

"Yes, but aren't some poisonous?" Violet asked nervously as the creature extended a tentacle slowly toward the mouselets.

"Let's get out of here!" Colette said anxiously. But before she could swim upward out of the current, a deep voice broke the silence.

"Please don't be scared," the voice said kindly. The jellyfish was speaking to them!

"We don't mean to bother you," Paulina said, gathering all her courage. "We're just on our way to Pink Pearl Castle to see Queen Anemone."

"What do you have there?" the jellyfish asked, pointing toward the stone in Paulina's paws with one of its TENTACLES.

"It's a Timekeeper Stone," Paulina replied.

The creature nodded. "Yes, of course," the jellyfish replied. "Then you must be looking for me, not Queen Anemone."

"Do you mean that you are the guardian of Aquamarina's Harmony?" Colette asked in surprise.

"Yes, I am," the jellyfish replied. "My name is Aurita. I am the oldest creature in AQUAMARINA. I live in the Infinite Abyss," Aurita explained. "My kind have forever guarded the most precious treasures of the sea. We watch over them at the bottom of the **ocean**, far away from danger."

"So we have to dive into the Infinite Abyss to get the Harmony, then?" Colette asked, **shuddering** with fear. She hadn't liked the abyss much on her last visit to Aquamarina.

"That won't be necessary," Aurita said. "I always carry the Harmony with me."

And with that, the jellyfish unfurled one of her long tentacles to show them the precious sphere. She passed it to Colette.

"Please be very **CAREFUL** with Aquamarina's Harmony," she told them. "It's the most precious object in the entire kingdom."

"Don't worry, we understand," Colette reassured the jellyfish. "We'll take good care of it. Thank you for your help, Aurita!"

"Best of luck, and thank you on behalf of all the creatures in the ocean," the

The Salt Shell
The Harmony of Honesty

A long time ago, a leprechaun named Argus lived in the Infinite Abyss. He worked in the salt mines at the very bottom of the ocean and spent his days sculpting amazing statues out of salt. One day while he was sculpting a seashell, the leprechaun heard a song coming from far, far away. It was a melody he had never heard before, and he was determined to find its source.

So Argus swam to the surface of the ocean, where he saw a mysterious creature sitting on a rock, singing. It was the prettiest nymph Argus had ever seen. As soon as she noticed Argus watching her, the nymph stopped singing. She took one look at the leprechaun and the pair fell in love.

Argus gave the nymph the salt seashell he had been carving as a token of his affection.

"Sweet nymph, I give you this seashell as a symbol of my love," he told her. "If you come down to the abyss with me, we will be happy forever!"

Blinded by love, the nymph followed him. But once she reached the bottom of the ocean, she began to miss the world at the ocean's surface. Every day she spent in the abyss, her heart grew sadder and sadder.

Argus realized what was going on and understood that the nymph was very unhappy.

"My dear, I cannot bear to be the reason for your unhappiness," he told her honestly. "You must go to the surface and sing again, even if it means we have to be apart."

The nymph offered to return the salt seashell to him, but he insisted she keep it as a reminder of their love. Ever since that day, the delicate seashell has been a symbol of honesty and respect.

jellyfish replied. Then she swam deeper into the sea, waving good-bye with her long, flowing tentacles.

"Now we have the *Harmony* from Aquamarina!" Paulina cheered.

"Yes, and that means it's time for our next RiDDLE," Nicky added as she unfolded the map again.

Pam read and reread the riddle a few times, scratching her head.

"To be honest, mouselets, I can't make HeaDS or tails of this!" she said sadly.

To get to the Land of Clouds, follow
the creatures with voices fine.
The ocean air will lead you to the
garden where many lights shine.

AQUAMARINA

LAND OF CLOUDS

"I think I understand the first part," Paulina said. "The Emerald Sirens are known to have very fine — and **DANGEROUS** — voices."

"That's true," Violet agreed.

"But I don't understand where we'll find a garden deep in the ocean," Colette continued. "That doesn't make much sense to me."

"We could try going to Sirens' Bay," Pamela suggested. "Maybe we'll find the gateway to the Land of Clouds there.

"Good idea!" Violet agreed.

So the five friends swam toward Sirens' Bay, home of the Emerald Sirens.

SiReNS' BAY

From a distance, the Thea Sisters could see the pretty houses along Sirens' Bay. As they got closer, they could make out the elegant SIRENS swimming around the sparkling waters.

"Remember: We cannot listen to the sirens' songs," Paulina reminded her friends.

"Right," Colette agreed. "The Emerald Sirens are tricky. Their song allows them to capture anyone who hears it!"

"We must be careful," Violet said. "If the sirens begin to sing, cover your ears as fast as you can."

The Thea Sisters nodded in agreement as they approached the village. Time was running out, and they had to find the magic gateway to the Land of Clouds as quickly as possible.

"Hello, dear mouselets." A siren with

flowing red hair greeted them. She was sitting on a mother-of-pearl bench, weaving small baskets from purple seaweed.

"Hello to you, kind siren," Colette replied.

"What are you looking for?" the siren asked with a sly smile.

"How do you know we're looking for something?" Pam replied, suspicious.

The siren's smile grew wider.

"I was **WATCHING** you," she replied coyly. "I can tell that you're new around here. Ever since you entered the village, you've been studying that map."

The mouselets glanced at one another. They knew they had to trust her.

Hello!

What are you looking for?

"We are looking for the ocean air," Nicky replied hesitantly.

The siren's eyes opened wide. Then she threw back her head and burst out laughing.

"Did I say something funny?" Nicky asked in surprise.

"The ocean air is EVERYWHERE!" the siren explained, spreading her arms open wide.

"But isn't there a specific place we can find it?" Violet asked. "A place that might lead to a garden, perhaps?"

The siren shook her head, looking confused.

"I'm not sure I understand what you mean," she answered.

At that moment, a royal seashell carriage led by a pair of *marine seahorses* approached. Esmerelda, the beautiful queen of the sirens, was sitting inside the shell.

"What a nice surprise!" the queen greeted

the Thea Sisters, her piercing blue eyes gazing at them. "What brings you back to Sirens' Bay, my dear friends?"

"Do you know these mice, Your Majesty?" the red-haired siren asked in surprise. "They are LOOKING for the ocean air . . . and a garden!"

"I see," the queen said, nodding. "And where is the handsome **Will Mystery** this time?"

Paulina and Violet exchanged a glance. It was no surprise that Queen Esmerelda remembered Will Mystery. She had tricked him into dancing with her on their last visit, and she had almost imprisoned him with her song.

Where is Will Mystery?

"We don't know where he is," Violet replied.

143

"We were hoping he might have passed this way before us," Paulina said.

"I would have liked that very much," ESMERELDA replied. "But no, he hasn't been here recently."

"We really don't have much time," Paulina said, bringing the conversation back to their mission. "All the fantasy worlds are in great danger!"

"Yes, we are searching for the 'garden where many LIGHTS shine,'" Nicky explained. "Please, can you help us?"

Esmerelda sang her reply:

"To get to the hidden garden, don't look very far . . ."

The Thea Sisters immediately put their paws over their ears so they would not be affected by the DANGEROUS siren queen's song. They would have to read her lips as she sang.

But the queen stopped singing immediately.

"If you don't listen to me, you will never find what you are looking for," Queen Esmerelda said with a smile.

It was clear then that Esmerelda knew where the mysterious garden was. But the Thea Sisters also realized they would have to listen to the song to find it.

In order to complete their **mission**, the mouselets would have to listen to the siren's song and fight its **POWER**.

The five friends reached out to hold paws while the siren sang. They knew they had to have courage and remain strong if they were going to make it.

While Esmerelda sang, Violet felt pulled by the enchanting **music**. She took a few steps toward the queen and was about to LET GO of her friends' paws. But the other Thea Sisters

To get to the hidden garden,
don't look very far.
You'll find the things you need are
close to where you are.
Flashing lights surround the seaweed
that floats by;
Follow the sea's foam from water
deep up to the sky.

held on tightly and kept their friend from giving in to the power of the SONG.

Suddenly, the queen was quiet. She looked at the mouselets for a long while before she finally spoke.

"You five are very special," she said. "I admire your friendship. It is a gift that gives you strength. You have proved yourselves to me, and I would be happy to take you to the place you are searching for."

"Thank you!" the mouselets cried gratefully.

Esmerelda climbed out of her carriage and swam gracefully toward the village. The Thea Sisters followed closely until they reached a beautiful underwater seaweed garden. It was

illuminated by dozens of glowing fish.

"This must be the **garden** where many lights shine!" Pam exclaimed as she watched the bright creatures dart among the plants.

"And these must be the ocean air!" Violet said, pointing to three underwater **geysers** spouting bubbly water up toward the surface.

"Should we follow the **SEA'S FOAM**?" Nicky asked Queen Esmerelda.

The queen nodded.

"**Good luck**, brave mouselets," she called after them as they swam away. "I hope to see you again soon!"

Paulina waved good-bye and turned to her friends.

"Let's go!" she said, and she immediately swam upward, following the bubbles and sea foam that would lead them through the gateway to the **Land of Clouds**.

THE WELL OF TRUTH

The Thea Sisters swam through the salty sea foam until they saw a bright light ahead of them.

"Here we go!" Paulina exclaimed happily as she popped up from the bubbling water to find herself standing in front of the magnificent **Cloud Castle**. She and her friends had just crossed the magic gateway that led from Aquamarina to the Land of Clouds!

"It's even more beautiful than I remember," Violet said, with a dreamy look in her eyes.

"Welcome back!" came two nearby voices. "We are happy to have you as our guests once again."

The Thea Sisters found themselves facing two smiling fairy guardians.

"Thank you, it's nice to be back!" the Thea

Sisters replied, happy to have arrived in the next **kingdom**.

"Would it be possible for us to see Queen Nephele, please?" Nicky asked.

"Of course," the first fairy replied. "She's in her private garden. Follow us!"

The fairies led the mouselets inside the castle. The great hall was exactly as

the Thea Sisters remembered it: The unique, elegant furniture and decorations had been created by the fairies from Clouds!

The mouselets followed the fairies along a wide, bright hallway until they finally reached the queen's garden.

"Your Majesty, you have visitors," the fairies announced.

Queen Nephele turned toward the Thea Sisters and recognized them immediately.

"My dear friends, how nice to see you!" she exclaimed, hugging each mouselet in turn. "Unfortunately, I know why you are here, and I know it isn't something to celebrate."

"You know about our mission, Your Majesty?" Paulina asked, surprised.

"Yes," Queen Nephele explained. "The Grand Council of Fairies told me about the MISSING Mayhem Mirror and about your imminent arrival in the Land of Clouds."

"We're working hard to stop the Fog of Fury," Colette said. "Our MISSION is to gather each kingdom's Harmony so that we can defeat the mirror and its evil spell."

Queen Nephele

"We are all in great danger, and you mouselets are the only ones who can save us," Queen Nephele said. "I see that Will Mystery is not with you, though."

"I'm afraid he's traveling separately," Nicky replied. "We know he's in the fantasy kingdoms as well, but we haven't heard from him in a while."

"I thought we would have run into him by now," Paulina said, sighing sadly. "I hope he's okay. What if something happened and he needs our **help**?!"

Queen Nephele looked at Paulina closely. She realized the mouselet was very worried. Putting her hand on Paulina's shoulder, the queen made a generous offer.

"You may ask the **Well of Truth**," she said softly. "Its water comes directly from the Spring of Truth. If your soul is pure, the well will whisper the **ANSWER** to you."

"What do you all think?" Paulina asked her friends. "Should I try it?"

"Of course!" Nicky said, hugging her friend tightly. "We all want to make sure Will is okay."

Paulina approached the well slowly. She leaned over the pool of water, gently placing her paws on the side of the well. Then she closed her eyes and asked her questions softly. A moment later, she turned to her friends to tell them what she had heard.

"The well replied with just ONE word," Paulina said. "**ARVIN**."

Queen Nephele's face grew pale.

"What is it, Your Majesty?" Violet asked. "Who — or what — is Arvin?"

"Arvin is a knight with a very complicated history," the queen replied.

"What is the story?" Paulina asked.

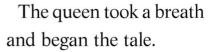

The queen took a breath and began the tale.

"Arvin was a very **brave** and **FEARLESS** knight," she explained. "The Grand Council of Fairies knew he had a NOBLE and trustworthy soul, and they gave him the very difficult task of taking the Mayhem Mirror to the ENDLESS VOID."

The Thea Sisters nodded. They had already heard some of the **story** from Aphelia. Now they finally knew everything. They had a feeling the story didn't end there, though.

Arvin

"Arvin completed his **mission**, but he recklessly broke the law along the way," Queen Nephele continued.

"Oh no!" Violet cried. "What happened?"

"He did it for love," the fairy queen replied. "Arvin took his beloved, a fairy named Fuchsia, all the way to the edge of the ENDLESS VOID. He wanted to show her the mirror, even though it was against the **RULES**."

"But why did he do that?" Colette asked, confused.

"Fuchsia was a 𝙲𝚄𝚛𝚒𝚘𝚞𝚜 fairy, and she loved adventures," Queen Nephele went on. "She asked Arvin to see the place, and he loved her so much he couldn't say no. The two of them were caught and found guilty by the Grand Council of Fairies."

"And then what happened?" Paulina asked.

"Arvin was 𝚎𝚡𝚒𝚕𝚎𝚍 forever.

Farewell, dear Fuchsia . . .

He moved to the Ebony Tower, which is beyond the borders of the Color Kingdom."

Arvin . . .

"What about 𝙵𝚞𝙲𝙷𝚜𝚒𝚊?" Pam asked.

"The poor fairy

wouldn't give up hope of finding him," Queen Nephele explained. "They say she is still looking for him *today*, though no one has seen her in many years."

"What a sad story," Colette said, sighing.

"There's more," the fairy queen went on. "Not long ago, some travelers told the Grand Council of Fairies they had seen a knight who looked very much like Arvin. But apparently this knight was a **lonely**, **DARK**, and unfriendly creature. There was no sign of the kind soul with the generous smile. I'm afraid that little by little over many years, Arvin may have given in to the mirror's power. Perhaps out of loneliness and desperation, I think he might be planning his revenge."

"But do you really think he went back for the Mayhem Mirror and plans to complete the witch's **curse**?" Violet asked in dismay.

"I don't know for sure," Queen Nephele replied, shaking her head. "But the *Well of Truth* just told us that Will is with Arvin, so anything is possible."

"Oh no!" Paulina exclaimed. "What if Arvin FOUND Will and is holding him prisoner?!"

"We have to find Will right away," Colette said firmly.

"But we also have to find the rest of the *Harmonies*," Paulina reminded her friends.

The queen's worried face grew even more serious.

"I'm afraid that won't be easy," she said, frowning. "You see, the Land of Clouds' Harmony has gone missing!"

THE BLUE FORTRESS

The Thea Sisters couldn't believe it. The Land of Clouds' Harmony was gone?

"Oh no!" Colette exclaimed.

"Ariel, the Harmony's guardian fairy, always carried the Harmony in a little cloth bag tied to her belt," Queen Nephele explained. "Just yesterday she was out flying with a friend. As they neared the Blue Fortress, they were caught in a terrible storm. The strong winds tore the bag from Ariel's belt. She and her friend looked everywhere, but the precious sphere had been **LOST**."

"How awful!" Pam said.

The queen nodded sadly. "Yes, Ariel feels terrible about it."

"What happens if the *Harmony* ends up in the wrong paws?" Colette asked the queen.

The queen shivered. "Oh, it would be horrible," she said. "But we don't think that will happen."

At that moment, a fairy entered the queen's garden. She handed the queen a white paper card.

The queen read the message and then turned to the Thea Sisters.

"It seems Ariel was spotted **flying** near the Blue Fortress again," she said, looking very worried. "I'm sure she is looking for the Harmony. But another **STORM** just blew in, and the winds are **WHIPPING** dangerously."

"What can we do to help, Your Majesty?" Paulina asked.

"*Come with me*," the queen replied. "We can't waste any time!"

She clapped her hands, and incredibly a

bunch of eagle-shaped clouds appeared in front of them.

"The **eagle-clouds** will take us to the Blue Fortress," Queen Nephele told the mouselets.

Following the queen's lead, the Thea Sisters climbed tentatively onto the clouds. At the queen's signal, the eagles' long, light silvery wings began to flap. Soon the group of friends was flying above the Land of Clouds in the ENDLESS blue sky.

"This new threat was very unexpected," the queen told the Thea Sisters as they flew. "The Land of Clouds had been having such a peaceful and joyous time. It's especially hard with King Nebus so far away . . ."

"King Nebus isn't at the palace?" Nicky asked.

The queen shook her head. "He is on a

t r i p to the far ends of the Land of Clouds," she replied. "He visits once a year to make sure everyone is doing well.

"That's the **SILVER CLOUDS TRAIL**," she said, pointing straight ahead. "It's the way to the Blue Fortress."

"Look!" Pamela pointed to a bright light in the clouds ahead. "What's that?"

"The fortress walls are made of **glowing** crystal," the queen explained. "They help light up the fortress in the dark and through stormy clouds."

Paulina checked the Timekeeper Stone as they flew. It was now between green and blue, and **flashing** regularly.

"According to the stone, the Harmony is nearby!" she said as they neared the pinnacle of the fortress, high in the DARK sky.

Rather than looking relieved at the news,

the queen looked dismayed.

"What's wrong, Your Majesty?" Colette asked.

"The strongest winds blow between those PEAKS," the queen replied. "The winds bring stormy weather and terrible rain. That's why this area is called the Stormy Vortex. I'm afraid the Harmony may be trapped in the winds created by the vortex."

The Blue Fortress!

"How will we be able to get it, then?" Colette asked in a *worried* voice.

The reply came from a new and unexpected voice behind them:

"Your Majesty, what an *honor* to have you at the Blue Fortress!"

It was one of the princes of Nimbus, and he was riding a winged unicorn, called an ungulate, with glowing fur. The prince smiled warmly at the mouselets and the fairy queen.

"*Prince Molton*, it's always a pleasure to see you all," Queen Nephele replied. "Unfortunately, we're here because our kingdoms are in danger."

"I think I know what it is, My Queen," Prince Molton replied. "The fairy Ariel told us she had lost the Harmony when we rescued her and took her to the fortress."

"Oh, I'm so glad to know Ariel is safe!"

Nephele replied. "Thank you."

"Now, please allow me now to help you retrieve the Harmony," Prince Molton replied, drawing his silver sword.

The queen and the Thea Sisters agreed. Then they followed the prince toward the **Stormy Vortex**. On the way, lightning lashed the dark sky as the wind howled around them.

"I think I can see the Harmony!"

Colette exclaimed suddenly. She pointed to the delicate sphere.

"You're right!" Pamela **SHOUTED** over the howling sound. "But the winds are blowing too hard. You'll never make it alone!"

"I can try to stop it with my sword," Prince Molton volunteered. "But I will only be able to do it for a minute or so."

"That will be good enough," Colette replied confidently. "While you keep the wind away, I'll fly as fast as I can to get the Harmony."

The prince agreed, and Colette took off toward the Harmony, holding tightly to the eagle-cloud. She dodged bolts of lightning, determined to grab the sphere. Colette reached out her paw and snatched the Harmony just before a *GUST* of wind threw her off the eagle-cloud.

"Colette!" her four friends cried out.

Quickly, the prince's *ungulate* swooped under Colette and caught her just in time. One second later and the whirling wind vortex might have **SWALLOWED** the mouselet forever!

THE RAINBOW
RIBBON

"Thank goodmouse!" Pamela sighed in relief.

"Way to go!" Violet shouted. "You did it, Coco!"

"I would never have made it without Prince Molton's help," Colette said admiringly. She held the delicate **sphere** in her paws.

"It was my pleasure," the prince replied.

"Thank you," Queen Nephele told Colette. "Ariel will be so happy to hear that we found the Land of Clouds' Harmony."

"We'll make sure to let her know right away," Prince Molton agreed.

"Please take good care of it," Queen Nephele said. "It's very special. An old legend says that the silver top inside the Harmony created the very first cloud in our kingdom."

The Silver Top
The Harmony of Imagination

There was once a warlock named Gray Wizard who drew his power from thunder and storms. Every day, the warlock would spin a silver top, creating a terrible vortex that brought stormy winds and downpours to the fantasy kingdoms.

But one day, something unexpected happened: Some lightning and thunder grew beyond the wizard's control. No matter how hard he tried to harness their power, he couldn't do it. The storm was so fierce, it destroyed everything in its path.

In fact, the wind was so powerful that it began to carry the silver top away from Gray Wizard. Worried that he would lose his precious object and the source of his power, the wizard went after the top.

While searching for the top, Gray Wizard met an explorer fairy named Aria, who was flying nearby. The top mysteriously reappeared, and it spun straight toward the fairy! Aria opened up her hand and the top landed gently on her palm. Gray Wizard watched in surprise as the top began to draw a very thin line that quickly became a shining thread. In just a few minutes, the thread had created a soft pink cloud, the very first cloud in the amazing Land of Clouds.

"Wow!" Violet gasped. "It must be **ancient**!"

"Now that we have the Harmony, we have to get back to our mission," Nicky said as she opened Will's map. She read aloud the next riddle, which would lead them to the gateway to the Land of Minwa.

To reach the Land of Minwa, find the ribbon that's a rainbow. The place where sweet treats are baked will lead you to the snow.

LAND OF CLOUDS

LAND OF MINWA

"This one is really **EASY**, girls!" Pam explained, rubbing her tummy happily. "The gateway must be in Fairywing Village, land of the Color Pixies! Mmmm . . . they make the best cupcakes. I can still remember the ones we tried on our last visit!"

The Thea Sisters burst out laughing.

"Pam, I think you and your stomach had better **LEAD** the way!" Paulina joked.

"The Color Pixies do make delicious desserts," Queen Nephele agreed, laughing. "Good-bye, mouselets, and good luck on your journey!"

The Thea Sisters waved good-bye as their eagle-clouds flew toward the colorful Fairywing Village. As they flew, the Thea Sisters went over their progress.

"We have four *Harmonies* so far," Paulina reminded them.

"And we know Will has the one from the Starlight Kingdom," Pam added.

"So, we still need the ones from the Land of Minwa, the Land of Erin, and the Land of Colors," Nicky said.

"Right," Colette agreed. "That means we're more than halfway there. We can do this, mouselets!"

"Yes," Violet agreed, reciting her favorite cheer: "*One for all and all for one. Mice together, friends forever!*"

At that moment, the eagle-clouds arrived at Fairywing Village. The **MOUSELETS** thanked them and said good-bye to the unusual creatures. Then Pamela sniffed the air, hoping they were in the right place.

"Ah!" she cried. "There it is: the sweet smell of APPLE PIE! This must be it."

All around them were cute little houses perched

on colored clouds. Aromas of baked treats wafted from the **chimneys**.

Colette approached a familiar-looking house.

"Rosebud, are you there?" she called.

A pixie poked her head out.

"Hello!" she said cheerfully. "Pixies, look who came back for a VISIT!"

A second later, the pixies who lived in the houses on either side of Rosebud's cottage had **fluttered** over.

"It's the Thea Sisters!" Lilac cried happily. "It's great to see you again!"

"What a warm welcome!" Colette smiled.

"Would you like a snack?" Bluebell asked.

Pam was about to reply, but Paulina cut her off:

"You are very kind, but we're in a hurry!" she told them. "We're looking for a **RAINBOW RIBBON**."

"The rainbow ribbon only appears when we all laugh together," Lilac explained.

"It's really important," Colette said. "The fate of all the fantasy kingdoms depends on it!"

"Well, in that case, you'll need to tell us something funny!" Bluebell said.

"I've got one!" Nicky said. "What did the strawberry say when it heard its favorite song?"

Bluebell shrugged and glanced at her friends, but they shook their heads.

"Tell us!" Bluebell urged Nicky.

"That's my jam!" Nicky said.

The pixies all burst out laughing. A moment later, the clouds around Fairywing Village exploded into colorful ribbons that began weaving themselves together right before the Thea Sisters' eyes.

"It's a ribbon that's a rainbow!" Violet exclaimed.

"Thank you, dear pixies," said Pam.

"No, thank you," Lilac replied, still *giggling*. "You were very funny!"

Paulina checked the Timekeeper Stone. It was time to go. With one last look at the lovely Fairywing Village, the Thea Sisters began walking toward the **COLORFUL** rainbow ribbon.

THE FOREST OF THE DANCING PINES

The Thea Sisters followed the rainbow ribbon to a soft cloud. Soon they were walking through a thick fog, and the temperature began to drop steadily.

"**BRRRRR**," Colette shivered. "Based on this cold, I think we're getting closer to the Land of Minwa."

After a few more steps, a bright white light came over the five friends, and they found themselves standing in a **snowy** forest.

"This is no ordinary forest," Paulina noted. "Those are **pines**! Can you smell them?"

"I have a feeling we're in the **FOREST of the Dancing Pines**, where the tengu live," Violet added.

The Thea Sisters had met the birdlike tengu

on a previous visit to the Land of Minwa.

"Look, the pines are **DANCING**!" Pam noticed aloud, pointing to the waving branches. "That must be how this forest got its name."

"Yes," Nicky agreed. "And I wonder where the tengu are. We'll need their help to find the Land of Minwa's guardian."

"Yes, it's not EASY walking through all this thick snow and ice," Paulina complained. "I'd rather get a lift from a tengu!"

"I have an idea," Violet said suddenly. "Since the pines seem to be dancing, maybe the easiest way to walk through them is by dancing with them!"

"What do you mean, Vi?" Pam asked.

"Just close your eyes for a moment and listen to the *swishing sound* of the branches in the wind," Violet suggested. "Can you hear the rhythm?"

"You're right, Violet!" Colette replied. "I can hear it."

"If we move with the trees in the same RHYTHM, I think we'll find it much easier to move through this tightly packed forest," Violet said confidently.

"I think that's a **great** idea!" Pam agreed.

The Thea Sisters closed their eyes and focused on the trees' steady rhythm. Then they opened their eyes and began to dance, moving slowly along with the pines.

"I've definitely never danced like this before," Colette said.

"It feels strange, but really natural, too!" Nicky said, smiling to herself.

The mouselets continued their dance until dark SHADOWS swooped down from the sky above.

"Hello, Thea Sisters," a tengu greeted them. "What a surprise!"

He flapped his large red wings and hovered in midair above them.

There were other tengu with him.

"It's so nice to see you again!" Paulina replied.

"How can we help you?" another tengu asked.

Colette quickly explained the situation.

"We don't have much time left to find the Land of Minwa's Harmony," she concluded. "Can you help us?"

"Of course," one of the tengu replied. "We don't know who the guardian is, but if you tell us where you're going, we would be happy to take you."

"You can always count on us," said another tengu. "We will never forget how you helped us when we could no longer fly. We will be forever thankful."

"We were glad to help!" Nicky replied, remembering their mission in the Land of Minwa, which had taken place so long ago.

"The Timekeeper Stone is flashing and pointing in that direction," Paulina explained, pointing north.

"The Crystal River is that way," the first tengu said.

The Thea Sisters knew what that meant: They would be visiting the **kitsune**!

THE HiDDEN
ENTRANCE

Each tengu grabbed one of the Thea Sisters and lifted her into the air. As they flew over the snow-covered Land of Minwa, they soon saw the Crystal River below them. The cold *water* flowed noisily through the mountain peaks. Everything was exactly the same as the mouselets remembered from their last visit.

The tengu steered gracefully toward the rock wall on one side of the river, landing near a plunging waterfall.

"Thanks for your help, dear friends," Colette said. "Now we have to find the kitsune."

"We are happy to have helped you," one of the tengu said. "You will find the kitsune in their **home**, which is hidden behind the waterfall. We cannot get any closer to the icy

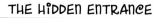
water or our wings will **FREEZE** and we won't be able to fly."

"You have done more than enough by bringing us to this point," Pam said thankfully. "We can continue from here on our own."

The tengu nodded and waved good-bye to the Thea Sisters before taking off, and the mouselets watched as they disappeared into the white sky.

Good luck!

"We were lucky to see the tengu when we did!" Pam remarked.

"Yes, but we'd better get moving," Paulina reminded them. She pointed to a place in the rock wall ahead of them that had tall steps carved in the ice. "I'll bet that's the *entrance* to the kitsune's home."

"I'll go first," Nicky volunteered, and she began climbing the icy steps, taking care not to slip on the smooth, slick surface. Her friends followed closely behind her, and soon they had all made their way to a narrow snow-covered ledge that jutted behind the thunderous *waterfall*.

Paulina pulled out the Timekeeper Stone from her pocket. It was flashing a deep **indigo**.

"This must be it," Paulina said, stepping behind the waterfall. The Thea Sisters followed. They had finally arrived at their *destination*!

They found themselves inside a warm, welcoming space. Glowing golden lights lit the palace, which the Thea Sisters knew belonged to the **kitsune**, tall, beautiful fairies with long foxlike tails.

"It's lovely in here," Colette said softly.

"I'm glad you like it!" came a reply. The mouselets turned to see one of the kitsune with a glowing golden sphere in her hands. The Thea Sisters knew the **mysterious** spheres were the source of the kitsune's powers.

"Hello," Violet said. "You may remember us from our previous visit to the Land of Minwa. We are the **THEA SISTERS**, and we are here on an important mission."

"It's our pleasure to welcome you," the fairy replied nodding toward the Timekeeper Stone. "And I already know why you are here. Come with me."

The Thea Sisters followed her into a room where other kitsune sat Sketching detailed drawings of beautiful snow-crystal jewelry.

"Over here," the fairy said, leading the mouselets to a smaller room.

"Holey cheese!" Pam exclaimed, looking around.

The walls of the room were lined with glass cabinets that showcased hundreds of sparkly objects.

Please, come with me . . .

"Oh wow!" Colette exclaimed as she looked into the cases. "This jewelry is so unique and beautiful! It looks like everything has been sculpted out of ice."

"Yes," the fairy said, nodding. "We kitsune make everything by hand. Every piece is an original."

"They are really GORGEOUS!" Violet agreed.

"Thank you," the fairy replied. "We are very proud of our creations. And in addition to our jewelry, we also store another precious and fragile object in this room: the Land of Minwa's *Harmony*!"

She took a few steps toward one of the cabinets. Then she pulled on a pair of silver gloves and removed the delicate sphere from the shelf. She passed it gently to Paulina.

"The Land of Minwa's Harmony is special because it contains the lost copy of the *Book of Ice*," the fairy explained. "It is an IMPORTANT book that recounts our kingdom's oldest legend. Please take good care of it!"

"We will," Paulina replied solemnly. She could feel the weight of the precious sphere in her paws.

Book of Ice
The Harmony of Friendship

A long time ago, a happy young nymph lived in the Land of Minwa. She loved to spend her days singing sweet melodies. One day while taking a walk, she ran into a mean witch in disguise. The witch stopped the nymph.

"Why are you so happy today?" she asked.

"I am always happy!" the sweet nymph replied, smiling.

"Happiness should be banished from the kingdom!" the witch cried with a scowl. Then she cast a spell on the nymph, and happiness disappeared from the young creature's heart.

The matter was brought to the attention of the Grand Council of Fairies. They revealed that the only antidote to the witch's spell was found in the *Book of Ice*, which was guarded by a frightening giant who lived in the mountains.

The nymph set out for the mountains immediately, for she was determined to get her lost happiness back.

Once she found the giant, she told him what had happened. He was unmoved by her story. Still, the nymph persisted. After much convincing, the giant allowed her to consult the precious *Book of Ice*. But the nymph could not open the book because its pages were frozen shut.

Day after day, the nymph tried to open the book, with no luck. Every day the giant watched the nymph, and over time, the pair became friends.

Then one morning, the nymph realized that the layer of ice on the book had melted. She opened the book, leafed through the thin pages, and read the story of a special friendship between a sad nymph and a grumpy giant. After she read the tale, the curse was broken and her happiness returned! From that day on, the *Book of Ice* became a symbol of everlasting friendship.

THE ICE CANOE

Now that they had the Land of Minwa's Harmony, the Thea Sisters left the hidden palace behind the waterfall. Outside, snow was falling all around them.

"We only have two *Harmonies* left!" Paulina whispered, happily holding the newest Harmony in her paws.

"Yes, which means we still need to travel to the Land of Erin and the Land of Colors," Nicky agreed.

"Let's take a look at Will's RIDDLE," Paulina suggested, keeping an eye on the Timekeeper Stone.

The five friends took shelter from the storm under a rock ledge and unfolded the **map**.

"Oh no!" Nicky gasped. "We have a problem: The map is torn!"

Nicky held out the map to show them.

"We're **missing** the part where the riddle should be," Violet said.

"But how can that be?" Paulina asked. "Wasn't the map whole before?"

"I don't know," Nicky replied, shaking her head. "Maybe it happened while we were flying with the tengu."

"But how?" Colette asked, perplexed.

"Or maybe it happened while we walked along the **RIVERBANK**," Nicky guessed.

"Well, what do we do now?" Violet wondered aloud.

"Let's walk along the river and see if we can find it," Nicky suggested. The mouselets walked alongside the flowing water, carefully checking all around them for the scrap of paper.

The map is ripped!

After **WALKING** for a while, Colette's paws were getting cold.

"I'm starting to give up hope, mouselets," she said. "There's nothing but snow and ice here, and it's **SO COLD**!"

Suddenly, Colette stopped walking. She tried to take another step, but she found she couldn't move a muscle. It was as if her paws were trapped in the ice!

"Help!" she cried out. "What's going on? I can't move!"

What's going on?!

Violet hurried over to her friend. "Oh, Coco!" she said. "It must be the **Snow Fairies**!"

Sure enough, the Thea Sisters noticed two beautiful fairies with long, bright blue hair and snow-white skin on the other side of the river.

Please forgive us . . .

On their last visit to the Land of Minwa, some Snow Fairies had trapped them in the *ICE* when they tried to travel beyond the Crystal River.

"Kind Snow Fairies, we are the Thea Sisters," Paulina explained. "We've visited Minwa before, and we are back to *SAVE* the kingdoms."

"You are the THEA SISTERS?!" the fairies asked. "Please forgive us. We didn't recognize you! We know all about your mission."

One of the fairies waved her hand in the air, and Colette was able to move her paws again.

"Can we help you?" the other fairy asked.

"Yes, there is something you could do," Nicky said hopefully. "We are looking for a magic gateway to the LAND OF ERIN."

The Snow Fairies looked at one another, confused.

"We don't understand what you mean," the first fairy said.

Paulina held out the Timekeeper Stone, hoping that might help.

"Please, we have to get to the Land of Erin before the stone turns black," she said.

"I see," the first Snow Fairy said. "We are not **ALLOWED** to take you there, but we can give you what you will need to get there."

The fairies began to wave their hands over their heads, and a whirling **TORNADO** of ice formed in the air. A few seconds later, the spiral of snow and ice had transformed into a sparkling canoe.

"It's an **ice canoe**!" Pam exclaimed.

"We have to get in that?" Colette asked, worried. "Won't it melt?"

"Of course not," the first fairy said, smiling.

"It's magic ice," the second fairy explained. "You can trust us. This canoe will take you to the sea *faster* than anything else in the Land of Minwa."

"The sea?" Violet asked.

"Yes," the first fairy replied. "An old legend says the magic gateway to the Land of Erin is in the sea, right near the Leprechaun Cliffs. We've never been there, but we have heard of it, many years ago."

"Water cold, water clear, waters far, waters near . . ." the second fairy said cryptically as she waved good-bye.

"Thank you!" the Thea Sisters cried as the current of the Crystal River quickly swept them away from the Snow Fairies, down the river, and toward the sea!

BEYOND THE GREEN FOREST

When the canoe finally reached the shore, the Thea Sisters stepped out onto dry land. As soon as they left the boat, the canoe slowly melted away in the blue water.

The mouselets noticed that their surroundings had changed: They were no longer in the Land of Minwa. Instead, they found themselves along the leafy green shores of Emerald Lake, in the Land of Erin!

"How amazing," Violet said. "The magic gateway between the two WORLDS was in the water!"

"Now that we're here, we'd better **HURRY,**" Paulina said anxiously. "I have a bad feeling about Will. I think he needs our HELP! Follow me. The Timekeeper Stone is pointing this way."

Paulina led her friends through an emerald-green field and toward the forest.

"This must be the GREEN FOREST," Nicky said. "Can you smell that mossy earth?"

"It smells so good!" Pamela said, sighing.

The mouselets moved quickly through the trees. Soon the forest was so thick the sunlight was barely coming through the leaves. It became harder and harder for them

This way!

to make their way along the moss-covered path.

Paulina looked down at the Timekeeper Stone, which was glowing brightly.

"Oh no," she said. "I think I recognize this place: It's the Gray Swamp!"

"I hope we don't have to cross it," Violet groaned, thinking of the greedy treasure goblins she and her friends had encountered on their last visit to the Land of Erin.

"I'm afraid we do," Paulina replied, checking the stone again.

"Do you mean to tell me that the Land of Erin's Harmony is being guarded by those greedy, unpleasant creatures?" Colette asked in shock.

"I guess we have to find out," Paulina replied. "For now, all we know is that the Timekeeper Stone is pointing us in that direction."

When the mouselets reached the swamp's shore, they saw an empty landscape ahead of them.

"Ugh, it smells awful!" Colette cried, holding her nose.

The Thea Sisters had no choice but to walk through the mud and sludge as they followed the flashing light of the Timekeeper Stone.

They had just begun walking when a voice cried out.

"Who dares to walk through **my swamp**?" it said.

"**Your swamp?**" came a second voice. "No, it's mine!"

Who's there?!

When the Thea Sisters PEERED through some plants to see who was talking, they saw two goblins. They were treasure guardians, and they were arguing over the slimy water puddles full of weirdly shaped roots and strange plants.

"I don't know why they're fighting," Violet whispered to Nicky.

"I know," Nicky agreed. "This place is no PRIZE."

"It's mine!" shouted the first guardian.

"No, MINE!" the second one replied angrily.

Finally, Colette cleared her throat to get their ATTENTION.

"Excuse me," she said. "Could you stop arguing for a moment? We need your help."

The goblins stopped fighting and turned to the Thea Sisters as if noticing them for the first time.

This is my swamp!

No, it's mine!

"**Who** are you?" the first one barked.

"And what do you want?" asked the second.

"We are searching for the Land of Erin's Harmony," Paulina explained. "Are you two its guardians?"

The first goblin scowled at the mouselets.

"And what will you give us if we tell you where it is?" he asked **DEFIANTLY**.

"I'm afraid we have no treasures to give you," Nicky said seriously. "But our mission is to save the kingdom you live in. Surely the **safety** of the Land of Erin is the most PRECIOUS treasure, and worth your time."

The goblins exchanged a quick glance.

"Fine," the first one said. "We'll help you. The Harmony is here, but we are not its guardians."

"*Follow us*," the second goblin said, and he quickly led the way over the knotty roots that covered the swamp.

THE GOLDEN HARMONY

The two goblins moved swiftly through the **swamp**. The Thea Sisters followed closely, struggling to keep up, careful where they stepped.

"I don't want to know what kinds of **creatures** live in that **mud**," Violet said with a shudder as she hurried to catch up to Colette.

"I can't even imagine!" Colette agreed, a grim look on her snout.

Finally, the goblins came to a stop in the middle of the swamp.

"Well, here we are!" the first one said, smirking.

They had reached a small island. There was nothing on it but a single **ENORMOUSE** ash-colored tree.

"Holey cheese!" Pam exclaimed. "This poor tree has had a tough life."

Paulina nodded in agreement.

"Even the pine cones hanging from the branches are dry and **BLACK**," she said.

Colette shivered. She could feel goose bumps rising on her fur. She couldn't wait to get out of the Gray Swamp!

"Why did you bring us here?" Colette asked.

"Well, if you don't trust us, we'll be on our way," the second goblin said haughtily.

"No, no, of course we trust you," Paulina quickly reassured him.

The first goblin leaned over and knocked on a DOOR in the tree's trunk. A moment later, a small winged nymph with fiery red hair peeked out.

"YOU AGAIN?" the nymph complained. "Didn't I tell you to leave me alone?"

"Trust me, we have nothing to do with it this time!" the goblin replied. Then he pointed at the Thea Sisters. "These mouselets want to see you."

"That's right," the second goblin chimed in. "We just showed them the way here."

The nymph **IGNORED** the goblins and turned to the mouselets.

"Who are you?" she asked, curious. "And why are you looking for me?"

Paulina showed her the Timekeeper Stone. "We are here for the Land of Erin's Harmony," she said.

The nymph's eyes grew wide with **FEAR**. "The rumors are true, then?" she asked. "It's really happening?"

Violet nodded gravely. "Unfortunately, yes," she replied. "The **Mayhem Mirror** is once again a threat to the fantasy kingdoms, and only the eight Harmonies can break the spell!"

"And we don't have much time left," Colette added, pointing to the Timekeeper Stone.

The **NYMPH** flew up to one of the tree's branches, picked a dry pine cone, and took something from inside it. Then she flew back down to the Thea Sisters and held out her hand.

Here it is!

"It's the Harmony!" the mouselets cried in unison.

Thank you!

The nymph gently placed the delicate, transparent sphere in Colette paw. Inside it floated a small GOLD-LACE clover.

The Gold Clover
The Harmony of Courage

Once there was a dragon named Sparkle who lived in the Land of Erin. Sparkle lived alone on a magic island in the middle of a lake where he received few visitors. The dragon was often lonely, and he longed for a friend. One morning, Sparkle spotted a Lake Fairy flying over the island. Desperate for a companion, he trapped the fairy in a labyrinth of clover and vowed to always keep her near him.

Soon word spread throughout the kingdom that a dragon had captured a Lake Fairy. All kinds of creatures came from all over to rescue her, but none were able to do it. Finally, a brave knight came to the island. His heart was pure, and the magic creatures who lived on the island decided to help him. When darkness fell, a thousand fireflies showed the knight the way to the middle of the labyrinth, where he saw the fairy.

At that moment, Sparkle arrived. He carried a gold-lace clover, which he offered to the knight if he would allow the fairy to stay. But the knight refused.

"No!" he said, bravely standing up to the dragon. "I will rescue her, and there's nothing you can do to stop me!"

Sparkle recognized and respected the knight's courage.

"Brave knight, you have made a courageous decision," Sparkle said. "I will let you and the fairy go."

"Sparkle, your heart is so big and good," the fairy said to the dragon. "Come with us now and you will no longer be alone!"

So, the trio left the island together with their gold clover, the symbol of bravery and courage.

"Thank you so much," Paulina told the nymph.

"We promise to guard and protect it," Pam added.

"I trust you," the nymph replied with a hopeful smile. "Good luck on your quest."

"THANK YOU SO MUCH FOR YOUR HELP!"

the Thea Sisters told the nymph as they turned to leave. She smiled and with a flap of her wings disappeared back inside the trunk of the tree.

TO THE COLOR KINGDOM

When she was gone, the Thea Sisters realized they were on their own again.

"Those **greedy** little goblins left us to fend for ourselves!" Pam shouted.

"Maybe they had something important to take care of," Violet said.

"They could have **pointed us** toward the magic door before they took off," Colette grumbled.

"That's true, but I have a feeling they have no idea where it is," Paulina said.

"We'll just have to figure it out **on our own**, mouselets!" Nicky said encouragingly. She pulled out the map from her pocket and opened it.

"I hope we're **close** to finding Will,"

Paulina said hopefully as she leaned closer to the map to have a look at the next clue.

Nicky read the riddle aloud:

To go to the Land of Colors, first choose a sturdy cap.
Then twist the stem, hold on tight, and you will follow the map!

LAND OF ERIN

LAND OF COLORS

"This is the **STRANGEST** riddle of all of them," Violet said as she scratched her snout.

"Where are we going to find caps?" Colette wondered. "I don't see any hats around here, do you?"

Paulina shook her head. "It sounds like the caps have stems," she mused. "But that doesn't make any sense."

"Well, first things first," Colette said. "We have to get out of this **swamp**. The climate is really making my fur frizz."

The five friends looked for a way out of the murky water. Once they had reached an open field, they regrouped.

"Now what?" Pam asked. "Where do we go from here? We don't have any more clues, and we're running out of time."

Paulina glanced down at the Timekeeper Stone and was alarmed to see how **dark** it had grown.

It could be a shoemaker pixie!

Unsure of what else to do, the Thea Sisters continued on paw for a while. When they heard a *rhythmic* sound similar to a pounding hammer, they stopped.

"I wonder if that's a shoemaker goblin!" Paulina exclaimed. "Thea told us about meeting one during our last adventure in the Land of Erin."

"Maybe he can help us," Pam said.

"It's worth a try," Violet agreed.

The mouselets followed the sound until they came upon a little goblin sitting on a stump. He was hitting the heel of a shoe over and over again with a little **HAMMER**.

Shoemaker goblin

"Hello," Nicky said cheerfully.

"Good day!" the goblin replied.

"I'm wondering if you can help us," Nicky continued. "We're looking for a **CAP** and a **STEM** that twists."

The goblin just laughed.

"Why, just look around you!" he cried before he jumped up from his stump and *scurried* away.

"**Wait!**" Violet called after him. "Come back!" But the goblin was gone.

"How **UNHELPFUL**!" Colette exclaimed, sighing deeply.

"What do you think he meant when he said to look around?" Nicky wondered aloud, studying their surroundings.

"Well, look at these giant mushrooms," Pam said slowly. Sure enough, the five mouselets were surrounded by enormouse purple mushrooms.

"The mushrooms have a cap . . . and a stem!" Paulina exclaimed suddenly.

"But of course!" Colette squeaked happily, clapping her paws. "Paulina, you're a genius!"

"The riddle said to twist the stems," Paulina remembered. She stepped up to a mushroom and began to push on the stem as if unscrewing the mushroom from the ground.

But the plant wouldn't budge.

"Nothing seems to be happening," she said, disappointed.

"Let's try pushing the other way," Colette suggested.

It was hARd, but the mushroom's stem finally moved.

"It worked!" Pamela cheered as she pushed on her own mushroom stem. A second later, the stem and cap began to TAKE FLIGHT.

"Hang on, Pam!" Nicky cried out as her mushroom lifted off the ground.

Colette, Violet, and Paulina pushed their stems and then grabbed on tightly as the purple mushrooms took off. Soon they were soaring through the clear blue sky on their way to the Land of Colors!

in THE COLORFUL SAND

As they flew through the sky, colored bubbles suddenly appeared in the air all around the mouselets.

"How beautiful!" Violet gasped. "The Land of Colors is showing us a **warm** welcome."

"Mouselets, my paws are starting to slip," Colette called out to her friends. "I can't hold on to this mushroom stem much longer!"

"Me neither!" Nicky agreed. "Let's look for somewhere to land safely."

At that moment, a big orange **bubble** floated toward Paulina and wrapped itself around her. A second later, the mushroom dissolved, and Paulina found herself floating through the sky inside the bubble.

Within moments, Colette, Nicky, Violet, and

Pamela found themselves alongside Paulina inside different **COLORED** bubbles. The wind carried the bubbles along until they began a gentle descent.

The mouselets looked down and noticed a stretch of multicolored sand dunes that went on as far as the eye could see. As soon as the mouselets touched down in the sand, the bubbles evaporated.

"I've never seen such fine sand," Violet remarked as she picked up a blue pawful. "How I would love to explore this amazing place!"

"It is *beautiful*," Colette agreed with a wistful sigh.

"Yes, it would be AMAZING to explore," Paulina said simply. "But we can't forget that we are here on a very important mission!"

"You're right," Nicky agreed immediately. "What does the Timekeeper Stone tell us?"

Paulina held out the stone in front of her and the Thea Sisters gasped. The stone was so dark it was almost completely **BLACK**!

"Does this mean we're out of time?" Violet asked worriedly.

"I don't think so," Paulina replied. "We still have a little time left. But the Timekeeper Stone no longer seems able to let us know which way to go."

"Then I hope Will has already collected the Harmony from the Land of Colors," Nicky said.

"We can't be sure, though," Colette replied.

"Mouselets, look!" Violet called suddenly. "The placement of the colored sand isn't random."

"You're right, Vi!" Pam agreed. "It looks like the sand forms geometric patterns."

"And it looks like the pattern is concentric circles," Violet noted.

"All the colors seem to come together," Nicky pointed out.

"Do you think the Harmony might be buried in the sand?" Paulina asked.

"I suppose it's possible," Violet said. "We don't have any other clues, do we?"

"You're **RIGHT**, we don't," Paulina agreed. "I think it's worth trying!"

The Thea Sisters followed the pattern. It was difficult to walk because their paws sank into the sand up to their ankles.

Suddenly, they heard a voice.

"Help!" came the cry. "**HELP ME!**"

"Did you hear that?" Colette asked.

"Someone is in trouble, come on!" Nicky exclaimed.

The mouselets followed the sound out into the middle of the sand dunes.

There, they saw a beautiful fairy with long

hair and big blue eyes. She was buried in the sand all the way up to her waist.

"Someone finally heard me!" the fairy said, her voice full of relief. "I've been calling out for such a long time!"

"We're here now," Colette said reassuringly. "And we'll help you!"

Nicky immediately began to rummage in her backpack. She quickly pulled out a rope, which she tied around her own waist. Then she passed the other end of the rope to her friends.

"Hold On to it as tightly as you can," she told them.

"Of course!" the Thea Sisters replied in unison.

Nicky very carefully took a few steps closer to the fairy. With each step, she felt her paws sink **deeper** into the rainbow-colored sand.

"This must be quicksand!" Nicky said.

Nicky got to her knees and reached out to the fairy.

"I'll get you out, don't worry," she said confidently. "Grab my paw and don't let go!"

The fairy reached out her hand to Nicky, and the mouselet pulled the fairy toward her.

"Okay, mouselets," Nicky called back to her friends. "Now pull!"

We'll get you out!

Thank you!

The Thea Sisters used all their STRENGTH to tug on the rope, and finally they pulled both Nicky and the fairy to safety.

"We did it!" Colette exclaimed.

"Are you okay?" Violet asked the fairy.

"Yes, I am now, thanks to all of you," the fairy replied, smiling gratefully.

"What happened?" Paulina asked, curious. "How did you end up in the quicksand?"

"It's a LONG story," the fairy said.

FUCHSIA'S STORY

The Thea Sisters were very curious to learn more about the fairy.

"First of all, let me introduce myself," she began. "My name is **Fuchsia**."

The mouselets couldn't believe **I am Fuchsia!** their ears. The fairy they had just rescued was the one Arvin had FALLEN IN LOVE with! Fuchsia was the fairy who had asked him to show her the Mayhem Mirror and the Endless Void even though it was prohibited.

"You're the fairy who fell in love with the knight Arvin?" Colette asked.

The fairy looked surprised. "Do you know Arvin?" she asked, blushing.

"We've never met him, but we've heard

about him," Colette explained. "We know he was given the **IMPORTANT TASK** of bringing the Mayhem Mirror to the Endless Void."

"And we also know what happened afterward," Violet added softly.

The fairy hung her head sadly. "Arvin is a brave and good **KNIGHT**," Fuchsia said. "He carried out his task successfully. What happened afterward was entirely my fault."

"Why do you say that?" Paulina asked.

Tears began to roll down Fuchsia's face. "I . . . I insisted on seeing the mirror," Fuchsia sobbed. "And now my beloved Arvin is being *punished* for my mistake. I will never forgive myself!"

"Please don't cry," Violet said gently, placing her paw on the fairy's shoulder. "It won't help. All you can do is think of the **future**."

"I've tried," Fushcia said. "Truly I have. I

believed in the power of our love, and I was ready to follow Arvin anywhere, even in exile. But I've been searching for him everywhere with no luck. And then I came here and I got trapped in this colorful quicksand!"

"You really haven't seen Arvin since he was exiled?" Paulina asked.

"No," Fuchsia replied, shaking her head. "I miss him so much. Perhaps you can help me find him?"

I've been looking everywhere . . .

"Well, to be honest, we are looking for him as well," Colette explained. "We're sorry to bring bad news, but there's something else you should know."

"We have reason

to believe Arvin took the Mayhem Mirror," Nicky continued.

"We think he is determined to destroy the kingdoms by releasing the FOG OF FURY," Pamela finished quietly.

Fuchsia went as pale as a slice of mozzarella. "No!" she cried out. "That's impossible!"

Colette held the fairy's hand. "I know it's difficult to hear," she said. "But Arvin is the only one who knew exactly where the mirror was and what it could do."

Fuchsia shook her head. "The thought that the knight I love would do something like that is breaking my heart." She sighed sadly.

"We can imagine how you must feel," Paulina said. "But you have to trust us. We are on a mission to save the kingdoms."

"We really need to find the Land of Color's Harmony," Pam clarified. "Once we have it, we hope to be able to break the mirror's **spell**."

"I can help!" Fuchsia said, SMILING for the first time since they had met her. "I know where the Harmony's guardian lives."

"Perfect," Colette said. "First we'll find the guardian, and then we'll head straight to the Ebony Tower."

"Yes, and we'd better hurry," Paulina said, showing everyone the dark Timekeeper Stone.

"Why the Ebony Tower?" the fairy asked, shuddering.

"We've been told Arvin is there now," Paulina replied.

"I see," Fuchsia said, her wings drooping sadly. "We'd better go, then."

Without another word, she led the mouselets out of the color dune desert to a field covered in yellow flowers.

"We're almost there," Fuchsia said. "The

Hue Fairy lives at the end of this gravel path."

"Who is the Hue Fairy?" Nicky asked.

"She is the **wisest** fairy in the Land of Colors," Fuchsia explained. "She knows every detail of all the legends from our land, even the oldest ones."

The Thea Sisters saw a strange building on the horizon. It was snowy white and shaped like a cone.

"That's it," Fuchsia said, pointing. "That's her home. The Hue Fairy spreads new **colors** from the top of the tower every day."

"Wow!" Paulina gasped in surprise. "How beautiful!"

Fuchsia and the mouselets approached the front door and knocked. A moment later, the door opened and a small fairy appeared. She was wearing a ruffled white dress and had white flowers in her hair.

"Fuchsia!" the fairy said WARMLY. "It's been so long since I've seen you!"

Fuchsia briefly explained what had happened and then asked the Hue Fairy about the Harmony.

"Is it still here?" she asked hopefully.

We are looking for the Harmony!

It's not here anymore . . .

The fairy shook her head. "No, I'm afraid it isn't," she explained. "A young ratlet visited me and showed me the Timekeeper Stone, so I gave it to him."

"Will has already been here!" Paulina exclaimed with relief.

"Yes, that was his name: **Will Mystery**!" the Hue Fairy confirmed.

"When was he here?" Colette asked.

"I'm not sure exactly when it was, but it's been some time now," the fairy replied.

"Did he look okay?" Paulina asked, her voice full of concern.

"Yes, he was fine, though he seemed very worried," the fairy replied.

"We think he may have met Arvin in his travels," Colette explained to the fairies. "Arvin may have captured Will."

"I just can't imagine the knight I love doing

something like that!" Fuchsia said.

"Unfortunately, dark magic can change anyone," the Hue Fairy said to Fuchsia. "But don't forget that love is a powerful antidote to dark magic as well, so all is not lost!"

"We have reason to believe Arvin is in hiding in the Ebony Tower, and we're heading there now," Violet told the Hue Fairy.

"Please be CAREFUL!" the Hue Fairy replied. "It's a dangerous place."

The Thea Sisters and Fuchsia thanked her for her help. Then they began their journey toward the northern border of the Land of Colors. That was where they would find the

dark,

isolated

Ebony Tower.

The Sphere of a Thousand Colors

The Harmony of Wisdom

A long time ago, a wise king with three beautiful daughters ruled the Land of Colors.

On each daughter's sixteenth birthday, the king gifted her with a ring. He explained that each ring contained a bit of the powers of the Land of Colors. Each sister was delighted with the special gift, and each girl vowed to cherish her ring always.

At first the sisters were happy sharing their powers, each a master of her own ring. Until one day a new emotion grew between them: envy. The three sisters argued over who was the most powerful and who deserved to take over the kingdom after their father retired. This went on for months until, one night, the middle sister took action. Tired of having just a bit of the power, she stole her sisters' rings, confident that if she wore all three, she would be the most powerful of them all.

But the three rings together unleashed such an intense light that the girl was overwhelmed. She fainted instantly, falling to the floor.

Her sisters found her, and they called the king. He picked up his daughter and carried her to her chamber so that she could recover. Then he took the three rings, held them in his hand, and recited an old spell. When he opened his hand, the rings had been fused together into one shiny, bright, and colorful stone.

The king wisely declared that the sphere was too precious to belong to just three people.

"The power of this stone belongs to the entire Land of Colors and its creatures," he explained.

That day, the king appointed a guardian to protect the delicate and precious object, which became a symbol of wisdom and unity.

THE EBONY TOWER

Fuchsia and the Thea Sisters walked a long way through the colorful valley until they got closer to a very high mountain range.

"This is the Rock Mountain Range, one of the most ancient regions in our kingdom," Fuchsia explained. "Just beyond them is a desert where you can find the Ebony Tower."

"So, we have to cross these mountains?" Colette asked.

The fairy nodded.

"Let's head for those GREEN rocks," Fuchsia said, pointing. "The slope there is gentler."

"This landscape is **incredible**," Nicky remarked as she started to climb over the boulders. "I've never seen anything like it!"

Fuchsia led the mouselets to the top of the green rock where they saw the most amazing

This way!

view of the entire kingdom in its many glorious shades of color. But looming on the horizon was a tall tower of imposing **DARK STONE**.

"There's the Ebony Tower," Fuchsia said.

Her face fell as she looked up at the building. "The legends about that tower are just awful. I can't believe that my beloved Arvin lives there."

"We'll **FIND OUT** what really happened," Colette said reassuringly.

The Thea Sisters and Fuchsia finished the rest of their trek in silence. When they finally arrived at the Ebony Tower, they stood outside the entrance and stared up at it. Suddenly, a *gust of wind* pushed them against the door, which opened with a creepy creak.

"Just looking at it makes my fur stand on end!" Colette said, her voice trembling.

"Let me go first," Fuchsia offered. "I'll know it's Arvin if we see him."

The mouselets nodded in silent agreement and followed the fairy inside. As soon as they entered, the door slammed shut behind them with a **BANG**.

"It's even worse inside!" Paulina said as she looked around.

They were standing in **semidarkness**, and it smelled musty. The Thea Sisters and Fuchsia were trying to find their way when two huge winged creatures suddenly plunged down toward them, grazing their heads with their claws.

"What are those?" Violet squeaked in surprise.

"Oh!" Fuchsia cried out in alarm. "Those must be the famous **IRIDESCENT GRIFFINS** that guard the tower!"

"Watch out!" Nicky shouted. "There are more coming!"

Where are they taking us?!

Help!

"We have to hide!" Paulina exclaimed.

But there was no place for them to go.

"I think we're **TRAPPED**!" Pamela replied hopelessly.

Let go!

The mouselets defended themselves as best they could, but in the end the griffins prevailed. Each mouselet was carried up to the top of the tower in the grips of a griffin's **POWERFUL** claws.

"Help!" the mouselets squeaked as their paws lifted off the ground. But there was nobody there to hear their cries.

After a frightening flight through the gloomy tower, the griffins dropped the mouselets in a dark, cavernous room.

SOMEONE in a dark cloak was waiting for them there . . .

DARK FORCES
AT WORK

Dark laughter echoed throughout the chamber as the cloaked figure stepped out from the shadows, revealing his face.

"Arvin!" Fuchsia rejoiced. "It really is you!"

But the fairy stopped speaking as soon as she saw the expression on the KNIGHT'S face. It was as if he had never seen her before in his life!

"Well, well, well," he said coldly. "What do we have here? Some young mouselets and a little Color Fairy."

"**ARVIN**, it's me, Fuchsia!" the fairy cried out. "Don't you recognize me?"

"Should I?" came Arvin's

quick reply. "You fairies are all the same: vain and shallow. It's very hard to tell you apart."

Fuchsia's face crumpled when she heard those words, and a tear slid down her face.

"Don't listen to him," Colette urged the fairy. "I'm sure he doesn't really mean it. It's clear he's under a spell or an evil **CURSE**!"

"And who are you?" Arvin asked, whirling to face Colette. "What are you doing in my tower?"

"We are the Thea Sisters," Colette replied. "And we're here to stop you from making a terrible **mistake**."

"We want to help stop the Mayhem Mirror from releasing the Fog of Fury," Paulina went on.

Arvin burst out **laughing**. "You aren't the first ones to try to stop me," he replied. "In the end, you'll end up just like him!"

Arvin pulled aside a heavy curtain to reveal a hanging cage with a prisoner trapped inside.

"**Will!**" the mouselets cried.

"I see you know one another already," Arvin said dryly.

"Be **careful**!" Will called out to them. "He is under the mirror's spell. He could do anything!"

"You'd better listen to him, because he's telling the **truth**," Arvin said. "I'll carry out my plan, no matter what!"

"The mirror is over there," Will told the Thea Sisters, pointing behind him.

But Arvin grabbed it before the mouselets could do anything. He unleashed its **POWER**. The mirror lit up with a ray of bright light as the knight turned to point it at the mouselets.

"We have to get out of here," Fuchsia cried out, but she had just gotten the words out when the ray of light hit Colette and Paulina. The mouselets stumbled and fell.

"We're not scared of you!" Nicky shouted.

"Are you sure?" Arvin replied cruelly. He spun the mirror around, and a second later a **WALL OF MIRRORS** surrounded the mouselets, reflecting Arvin thousands of times.

"Oh no!" Colette cried. "We're surrounded!"

"Mouselets, what you see around you isn't real," Fuchsia reassured them. "It's just an illusion. Don't believe it!"

"Mind your own business," Arvin snapped angrily.

Then he turned the mirror and pointed it directly at Fuchsia. A bright **BLUE LIGHT** shot out of the mirror and hit her full force. Fuchsia fell to the ground and lay there, unconscious.

"What did you do to her?" Colette demanded, her eyes flashing furiously.

"She got what she deserves," Arvin replied

coldly. "And now it's your turn, mouselets. Nobody can stop me.

I WILL HAVE MY REVENGE!"

The mirror lit up once more, casting evil reflections around the room.

The Thea Sisters were in trouble. Even though they knew that the terrible images they saw had been created by the Mayhem Mirror and weren't real, they were having trouble controlling their fears. The mirror's **dark magic** had a hold on the mouselets' hearts.

A RISKY PLAN

Will Mystery watched the mouselets from the cage above. He had to come up with a way to help them! And then it came to him. Will searched his pockets and pulled out a BLACK hemisphere. It was the other half of the mouselets' *Timekeeper Stone*!

Making sure Arvin couldn't see him, Will waved his arms to get the Thea Sisters' attention. Finally, Paulina noticed him.

"Girls, don't look all at once, but Will is trying to tell us something," Paulina whispered.

"Will has the other *Timekeeper Stone*!" Nicky said.

Violet watched Will as he mimed tossing the stone to her. He gestured again, and she understood immediately.

"He wants us to throw him ours!" Violet said.

"Yes, but how?" Colette asked *nervously* as she looked from the cage to the mirror, which was still flashing, sending dark images all over the chamber. "It won't be easy to reach him up there."

"It's our only chance," Paulina said simply. "We at least have to try."

She pulled out the Timekeeper Stone and held it in her paws.

"You're right, Paulina!" Nicky said quickly. "We'll try to **DISTRACT** Arvin while you get closer to Will."

The Thea Sisters set their plan in motion. Paulina CAREFULLY edged closer to the cage while the others distracted Arvin. Meanwhile, Will shouted to the other mouselets so Arvin wouldn't focus on Paulina.

Pam moved toward Arvin to keep his attention.

"How dare you **CHALLENGE** me?" Arvin yelled angrily when he realized Pam wasn't backing down. "I will destroy you!"

"We'll see about that," Pam said.

"We've got your back!" Nicky whispered to Pam as Arvin raised the mirror above his head threateningly.

A moment later, a **BLAST** of bright light shot out of the mirror at Pam.

"Watch out!" her friends cried.

Pam jumped to the left and rolled onto her side to keep from getting hit.

"You were **lucky**," Arvin shouted, furious. "You won't get away from me next time!"

"Mouselets!" Colette said suddenly. "I think I have an **IDEA**. If we all move forward at the same time from different sides of the room, Arvin won't know who to attack first. He'll get **confused**!"

"Great idea, Coco," Violet agreed. "This way we'll buy some time for Paulina to get the Timekeeper Stone to Will."

The Thea Sisters *quickly* put their plan into action. Arvin didn't know what to do! He darted around the room, unable to figure out who to strike out at first.

In the meantime, Paulina had moved so that she was now just underneath Will's cage.

"I'm ready!" Will whispered to Paulina as he prepared to catch the stone. "On the count of three, throw!"

Paulina took aim.

"One, two . . . three!" Will cried.

The Timekeeper Stone flew from Paulina's paw, and Will reached out, grabbing it at just the right moment. Arvin turned and saw the stone soaring through the air. His eyes grew wide as he realized he had been tricked by the mouselets. But it was too late. The stone was safely in **Will's** hands.

"Stop right there! What do you think you're doing?" Arvin shouted.

A NEW BEGINNING

Will realized he had to act **quickly**, before Arvin had a chance to attack. Without wasting a moment, Will grabbed the two Timekeeper Stone hemispheres and pressed them together, like two halves of an apple. The two parts fit together perfectly, and the entire sphere began to flash with a warm, pulsing light. Then something even more remarkable happened: Inside the sphere, a beating heart appeared!

"Arvin!" Will called out.

Upon hearing his name, the knight turned around in surprise. The light from the glowing sphere in Will's hand radiated out toward the knight.

"Noooooo!" Arvin yelled as the light surrounded him completely. Will and the

Thea Sisters watched in DISBELIEF as the knight stared at the light, transfixed. Arvin's cold, hard eyes seemed to warm and soften. Before long, they were shiny with tears.

Arvin blinked the tears away, looking around the room in surprise. Suddenly, he noticed Fuchsia lying unconscious on the floor.

"Fuchsia!" he exclaimed in disbelief. "What happened?!"

He rushed to the fairy and knelt down beside her, repeating her name over and over again.

The Thea Sisters could hardly believe the knight's sudden transformation. Just a few moments earlier, Arvin's face had been contorted with cruelty as he prepared to unleash the mirror's evil curse. Now he was on his knees crying over his **lost love**.

After a few moments, the fairy slowly opened her eyes.

"Fuchsia!" Arvin cried with relief. "Fuchsia, look at me!"

"Arvin?" the fairy whispered softly. "My dear Arvin, is it really you? I've been searching for you for such a *long time*!"

"I looked for you, too!" Arvin said. "But let's put that behind us. All I ask of you now is for your **FORGIVENESS**. Everything that has happened has been all my fault!"

"No," Fuchsia replied, sitting up. There were tears in her eyes. "I asked you to let me see the mirror, so it was my fault, too. And now what matters most is that we stop the mirror from unleashing the Fog of Fury over all the kingdoms!"

Arvin looked from the Thea Sisters, Fuchsia, and Will to the mirror, which was lying on the floor.

"I've made a lot of **MISTAKES**," he said, his

face serious. "But I promise to do all I can to fix things!"

"You have to let Will go," Paulina said. "He came here to save the kingdoms. He doesn't deserve to be trapped in a cage!"

"Of course," Arvin said sadly. "Forgive me."

Then he walked to the stone wall and pushed aside one of the bricks to reveal a lever. He pulled the lever, and the chain that the cage was hanging from started to move with a creaking sound. The cage lowered slowly to the floor.

Once the cage came to a stop, the knight pulled out a key

This is a new beginning!

that had been hanging from a string around his wrist. He unlocked the cage, and Will stepped out to greet the Thea Sisters.

"Will!" Paulina shouted as she and her friends surrounded him in a giant hug.

"You're finally **FREE**!" Violet added happily.

Will hugged his friends one by one. "Mouselets, I'm so glad you're all safe," he said, relief in his voice.

"THANK YOU FOR COMING TO MY RESCUE."

"The Timekeeper Stones really saved us," Violet said. "Look at that bright, pure **light** coming from the joined hemispheres!"

Will and the Thea Sisters looked at the stones in surprise, *mesmerized* by the strength of the light.

"I had no idea the two connected halves would have so much power," Nicky said.

"Yes, the power of the two stones is one of the strongest forces of good in all the fantasy kingdoms," Arvin explained. "You will see what the stones can do, but first we have to take care of the **Mayhem Mirror**!"

THE NINTH HARMONY

Arvin strode across the chamber to the mirror, which lay on the floor in the corner. The others followed him, and the Thea Sisters saw the magic object up close for the first time. The mysterious **black pearls** sparkled in its metal frame.

"This is the most **POWERFUL** dark object ever made," Arvin explained.

"You were very brave to take it to the Endless Void," Will told him.

"Yes, but I was also very reckless when I agreed to let Fuchsia see it," the knight replied honestly.

"We all make **MISTAKES**," Paulina said.

"But I promise I will fix everything!" Arvin replied. "The only way to set things right is to break the mirror's curse. And there is only one way to do that: We must replace the 🄴🄸🄶🄷🅃 🄱🄻🄰🄲🄺 🄿🄴🄰🅁🄻🅂 with the Harmonies from the eight kingdoms. But I don't see how we'll ever get them all in time."

The Thea Sisters pulled out the six Harmonies they had collected during their journey and showed them to Arvin.

"We got a bit of a head start," Colette said, smiling.

"B-but these are . . . how did you get them?!" Arvin exclaimed, surprised.

"Well, we only have **six**," Paulina pointed out, looking hopefully at Will. Had he been able to collect the others?

Will grabbed his backpack and pulled out the Harmonies from the Land of Colors and the Starlight Kingdom. The first sphere contained a rainbow of thousands of colors, and the second one contained a sparkling crystal star.

"You did it, Will!" Violet exclaimed when she saw the last two Harmonies.

"Looks like between all of us we have what we need," Will said.

"I don't know how to thank you," Arvin told Will and the Thea Sisters, smiling happily. "Now we have to remove the pearls from the frame so that we can replace them with the Harmonies."

"Yes, but we must be very careful," Fuchsia said. "It could be dangerous. The pearls are full of EVIL magic."

"Let me do it," Arvin offered. "You have all

played your parts in this difficult mission by gathering the Harmonies from the eight kingdoms. Now it's my turn."

I have to be the one to do it . . .

"Are you sure?" Fuchsia asked, worried. "We don't know what will happen once they are taken from the mirror's frame."

Arvin took Fuchsia's hands in his own. "My dear Fuchsia, I need to MAKE UP for all my mistakes," he explained firmly. "I will not change my mind."

Fuchsia nodded. "I understand," she said. "But please be careful!"

"Everyone, step back and get ready to place the Harmonies in the frame after I remove the pearls," Arvin instructed Will, Fuchsia, and the mouselets.

Everyone took a step back, and Arvin CAREFULLY reached out and touched the first pearl. He pulled it out of its spot in the mirror's frame.

The mirror began to glow with a dark light, but Arvin kept going. He placed the first pearl gently on the ground and moved on to the next one.

Will, the mouselets, and Fuchsia waited breathlessly. No one knew for sure what might happen once the final pearl was removed.

When there was just one pearl left, Arvin took a deep breath.

"This is the last one," he said. "Be prepared for anything!"

The knight bravely stepped up to the mirror, and with a smooth motion he removed the final pearl. The moment the pearl left the frame, the mirror made a loud **rumbling** sound just like a crash of thunder. A dark bolt of lightning flashed from the mirror, striking Arvin in the chest.

The knight fell to the floor and lay there, **UNCONSCIOUS**, the dark pearls all around him.

"Arvin!" Fuchsia cried. "Oh no!"

She raced to his side and fell over the knight, sobbing.

"Will, what's going on?!" Paulina asked.

"It must be the mirror's **CURSE**!" Will explained.

"What can we do?" Nicky asked. "We have to help Arvin!"

"We must replace the pearls with the Harmonies," Will reminded them. "We have to trust that the mirror's curse will be broken if we finish the mission!"

The five friends nodded, looking at Fuchsia, who was still by her **sweetheart's** side.

"Quickly, let's get the Harmonies in the frame!" Paulina said. She, Will, and the other Thea Sisters got to work. Carefully, they placed each sphere in the mirror. Each time they placed one more Harmony, the mirror lit up with a warm golden glow.

"I think it's working!" Will said hopefully.

"I hope so!" Pamela said.

Finally, all the Harmonies were in place. The Thea Sisters held their breath as they waited for them to take effect.

"Nothing's happening," Colette whispered.

"Wait, this one is still MISSING!" Will replied, showing them the bright sphere made of the two Timekeeper Stones.

"Do you mean the two stones together make up a ninth Harmony?" Paulina exclaimed in surprise.

Will nodded. "Yes, and this is the most important Harmony," he replied. "It must be placed at the top of the mirror to activate its power to block the FOG OF FURY once and for all!"

"Let's hurry, then!" Pamela exclaimed.

Will nodded. "Shall we place the last *Harmony* all together?" he asked the mouselets.

"Yes!" they replied, and they took a step closer to help their friend.

Once the Timekeeper Stones had been placed in the frame, the edge of the mirror began to glow so brightly it was like a warm, delicate morning sun on the horizon.

They HAD DONe it!

THE POWER OF LOVE

"I can't believe we did it!" Paulina exclaimed, elated.

"The mirror's curse has been **broken**," Pam cried. "The fantasy kingdoms are forever safe from the Fog of Fury!"

"Hooray!" cheered the mouselets.

"You did an AMAZING job," Will congratulated the Thea Sisters. "It was the most difficult mission you've ever undertaken. I'm so proud of you."

"We're so glad everything turned out okay!" Colette said as she **sighed** in relief.

"Well, not quite everything," Violet said softly. She pointed toward Arvin and Fuchsia. The knight was still lying on the floor while the fairy sat beside.

"Oh no!" Nicky exclaimed. "What

happened? The spell has been broken, but Arvin hasn't woken up."

The Thea Sisters and Will moved closer to Arvin and Fuchsia.

"He's still unconscious," Will confirmed.

"I don't understand," Paulina said.

Fuchsia held Arvin's hand in her own. "My darling," she whispered as tears spilled down her face. "Please come back to me."

Colette put her paw around the fairy's shoulder to try to comfort her, but Fuchsia kept crying.

Suddenly, Paulina noticed something. As Fuchsia's tears fell, they formed a pool around the black pearls Arvin had removed from the mirror. As soon as the tears touched the pearls, they began to sparkle like small fireworks.

Then the black pearls began to **crumble**. Before long, they were nothing more than piles of black dust in a pool of the fairy's magic tears. Will and the Thea Sisters watched as a beautiful dragonfly with ruby-colored wings emerged from the dust.

"But that's impossible!" Violet exclaimed.

"It's so beautiful!" Colette said, her face full of wonder.

A second dragonfly followed the first, then a third, a fourth, a fifth, a sixth, a seventh, and an eighth. There was one for each black pearl that had been removed from the mirror.

While the Thea Sisters stared at the

dragonflies in awe, Violet noticed something.

"Mouselets, look!" she cried. "Arvin is **waking up**!"

The knight had finally opened his eyes. "Fuchsia, is that you?" he asked in surprise.

"Oh, Arvin, you're **OKAY**!" the fairy exclaimed as she threw her arms around the knight's neck.

"Wh-what happened to me?" Arvin asked. He was still feeling very confused.

"The **DARK POWER** of the Mayhem Mirror hit you when you took the last pearl out," Will Mystery explained.

"But now it's over," Fuchsia reassured him. "You removed the eight black pearls and the Thea Sisters and Will replaced them with the eight Harmonies!"

"It's true," Will confirmed. "The fantasy kingdoms have been saved."

Arvin gazed lovingly at Fuchsia.

"We can finally be TOGETHER again," he said, smiling. Then he knelt down on one knee in front of the Color Fairy and took her hands in his own. He removed the ring he was wearing and gave it to her.

"I've been wearing this ring for a long time. The mirror's dark magic would have kept me from doing this, but now that I'm free from its power, I have to ask you a simple question:

Well done!

Yay!

Fuchsia, will you marry me?"

The fairy looked down at the ruby ring and tears filled her eyes.

"Oh, Arvin, yes!" she replied. "I love you with all my heart and I would be happy to be your **wife**."

"Yay!" the Thea Sisters exclaimed as they clapped their paws.

PRISM THE RAINBOW DRAGON

Just then, the colorful dragonflies that had been flying around the tower flew out the window, one after another.

"Look!" Colette said, pointing to the dragonflies. "They're leaving."

The other Thea Sisters and Will rushed to the window to get a better look at the creatures as they flew toward the horizon. As if by magic, a beautiful RAINBOW stretched across the sky. It was the biggest and most beautiful one the mouselets had ever seen!

"How incredible!" Violet whispered.

"Our kingdom is so full of peace and beauty, isn't it, Arvin?" Fuchsia said with a sigh.

"Yes, it is," Arvin said. "I appreciate it more now after almost losing it — and you!"

"How romantic," Colette whispered to Nicky. "They're so **in love**!"

The two sweethearts held hands as they came toward Will and the mouselets.

"Dear friends, we don't know how to thank you for all that you've done," Arvin said.

"Wait, Arvin!" Fuchsia said suddenly. "We do know how to **thank** them!"

"We do?" Arvin asked, curious.

"We'll invite them to our *wedding*!" the fairy replied joyfully.

"Of course!" Arvin agreed at once.

"You helped Arvin and I find each other again!" Fuchsia added. "We thought we had lost each other forever."

"Fuchsia is right," Arvin said. "Inviting you to our wedding is the very least we could do!"

The Thea Sisters accepted the invitation *happily*. What an amazing way to end their **adventure** in the fantasy kingdoms.

The Thea Sisters hugged one another, full of excitement at the idea of attending the fairy and knight's wedding. It was sure to be a joyful, **MAGICAL** affair. Will Mystery looked on quietly, smiling at the **mouselets**. Without their help, he knew there was no way the mission would have succeeded!

"Let's head to **Chiaroscuro Castle**," Fuchsia said. "We have to tell the other fairies about the wedding and start planning!"

Fuchsia began to sing softly as if to herself. A moment later, the face of a colorful dragon appeared at the window.

The Thea Sisters leaped back from the window in ꢱꢿꢣꢣꢣꢣ.

"A dragon!" Paulina gasped.

"It's okay," Fuchsia quickly reassured them. "Don't be afraid. This is Prism, the Rainbow Dragon! He is a loyal friend of the Color Fairies. He will take us to the castle."

Fuchsia climbed out the window and onto

the dragon's back first. She spoke to the dragon gently and thanked him for answering her call.

Prism bowed slightly, and Fuchsia gestured to Will and the Thea Sisters that they should climb on, too. When everyone was ABOARD, the dragon took off, flying smoothly through the Land of Colors' amazing sky.

To the castle!

CHIAROSCURO CASTLE

As they flew on the dragon's back, Paulina asked Will what had happened to him on his journey.

"I'm so glad we found you," Paulina began. "But what happened? We were so surprised when we arrived at the Seven Roses Unit and you were nowhere to be found!"

"Yes, it was so unlike you," Colette agreed. "We were really worried."

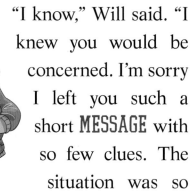

I know . . .

We were worried!

"I know," Will said. "I knew you would be concerned. I'm sorry I left you such a short MESSAGE with so few clues. The situation was so *urgent* I really had no other choice!

"I was given the Timekeeper Stone by the Grand Council of Fairies during one of my first Seven Roses Unit missions," Will continued. "I promised the fairies I would come to help them if the stone ever rang its danger alarm."

"We understand," Violet replied. "We just thought we would catch up with you at some point."

"But we missed each other because I came straight here to the Land of Colors from the Starlight Kingdom while you went in the other direction to the CRYSTAL KINGDOM," Will said.

"And then what happened to you?" Nicky asked.

"I found out about Arvin and tracked him down," Will said. "But when I finally found him, he was too powerful. He captured me and held me prisoner in the Ebony Tower."

"I hope one day you will forgive me, Will," Arvin replied.

"It's not your fault, Arvin," Will replied. "You were under the mirror's spell."

"What matters now is that it all **ENDED WELL**," Paulina said wisely as the majestic rainbow dragon neared the towers of Chiaroscuro Castle.

"But . . . the castle is black and white!" Violet gasped in surprise.

"No, it's **CHiaROSCURO**!" Fuchsia corrected her, reminding her of its name. "It's a study in shadow and light. And there's another secret to the castle: All the kingdom's colors are reflected in its walls. The **shades** change from one minute to the next."

"Look, it's true!" Violet said. She pointed at

the magnificent castle. "It looked peach for a moment, and now it's clearly lilac!"

"Now it's blue . . . now green . . . now black and white again!" Paulina said in awe.

"Holey cheese!" Pamela exclaimed. "It must have changed color ten times in the last minute alone!"

The next moment, the dragon began its final descent, landing gently in a *garden* full of bushes and trees that were bursting with leaves of every color of the rainbow.

The Color Fairies were waiting there, and they were wearing the most *elegant* evening gowns the Thea Sisters had ever seen.

"Fuchsia!" one of the fairies cried as she ran to hug the Color Fairy. "It's really you!"

"Azura!" Fuchsia said warmly. "I'm delighted to see all of you, too. These are my friends Will, Pamela, Violet, Colette, Nicky, and Paulina. I will tell you all the entire story soon enough, but for now, you should know that without their help, I wouldn't be here with you today!"

"Thank you from the bottoms of our hearts!" one of the fairies said gratefully.

"And that's not all," Fuchsia went on. "They saved all the kingdoms from the curse of the Mayhem Mirror!"

"You have our eternal gratitude," said another fairy as she bowed to the guests.

"The fantasy kingdoms are a precious and unique treasure," Will said. "We will protect them always!"

And with that, Fuchsia, Arvin, Will, and the Thea Sisters headed inside the castle.

THERE WAS A ROYAL WEDDING TO PLAN!

A WEDDING TO REMEMBER

On the day of the wedding, the Thea Sisters woke excited for the ceremony.

"We've been to many weddings in the fantasy kingdoms, but I have a feeling this one will be the most special one of all," Violet said to Colette.

"You're right," Colette agreed as she adjusted the pink gown the fairies had loaned her. "This party will be a celebration of Fuchsia and Arvin's love, and it will also **honor** the survival of all the kingdoms!"

"Isn't it incredible that the Grand Council of Fairies decided to throw eight parties in the eight kingdoms at the exact same time to celebrate the success of our mission?" Paulina asked.

"It will feel like every creature in every kingdom is at the **wedding**!" Pamela agreed.

"You two should try these on," Paulina said as she handed Pamela and Nicky two beautiful pieces of jewelry. "I think they'll look great with those gorgeous gowns."

"I must say that I think we look pretty fabumouse, mouselets," Colette added. "Don't you agree?"

"You've got that right!" Violet said as she adjusted her elbow-length lilac gloves.

Here, try these . . .

"I can't wait for the party to start!" Pamela squeaked happily.

At that moment, a fairy came to tell the mouselets to take their places in the *elegant* garden in the center of Chiaroscuro Castle. The ceremony was about to begin!

The sweet, soft strains of violin music filled the air, and Fuchsia and Arvin appeared. The Color Fairy was *radiant* in her beautiful pink silk-and-tulle dress. Arvin looked handsome and **REGAL** in his uniform and cloak.

The couple walked slowly down the aisle, smiling happily.

Then they stopped and turned to face each other. Finally, they held hands tightly and exchanged VOWS.

Everyone in the garden broke into loud cheers and applause, and the fairies ushered all the guests into the splendid IRIS HALL, where the celebration and dance party would take place.

Once the party was underway, Will asked Paulina to dance.

"I would love to," Paulina replied.

Will took the mouselet's paw and led her onto the dance floor where Arvin and Fuchsia were already dancing HAPPILY. The Thea Sisters looked on, smiling at their friend and the director of the Seven Roses Unit.

The celebration lasted well into the night. The fairies and their guests had a wonderful time celebrating the love of Fuchsia and Arvin, and the remarkable friendships that had brought the pair together at last.

The mouselets knew there was something different about the mission they had just completed.

"It feels like this mission marks the end of something **SPECIAL**," Violet said thoughtfully as she, Will, and her friends stopped at the castle gate to wave good-bye to the fairies.

"Farewell!" Fuchsia said, smiling brightly. "Thank you for everything."

With one last glance at the beautiful Land of Colors, Will and the Thea Sisters boarded the Crystal Elevator for the return trip to the *Seven Roses Unit*.

Before they knew it, the Thea Sisters were back on the ultrasonic helicopter and speeding toward Whale Island and Mouseford Academy.

When the mouselets got off the helicopter, the pilot handed them a mysterious *package*. The mouselets quickly unwrapped it to reveal a folded piece of parchment.

"It's the Magical Gateway Map!" the mouselets exclaimed in surprise. But when they unfolded it, they realized that strange marks had replaced the passageways between the kingdoms, creating a unique image.

"It looks just like a flower!" Violet exclaimed in surprise.

"No, it's not a flower," Colette said. "It looks like a precious gemstone!"

"I think you're both wrong," Pamela said confidently. "It's definitely a snowflake."

Inside the package there was a note from Will Mystery. It read:

Dear Thea Sisters,

The image on this map shows your limitless imaginations and shows the power of the stories that created the fabulous fantasy kingdoms.

Until next time . . .   —Will Mystery

The Thea Sisters read the note and hugged one another happily. They knew that from that day forward their **AMAZING ADVENTURES** in the eight fantasy kingdoms would live on forever in their hearts!

Hooray for the power of imagination!

Thea Stilton

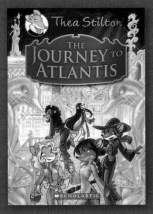

Secret Fairies

Don't miss any of these exciting series featuring the Thea Sisters!

Treasure Seekers

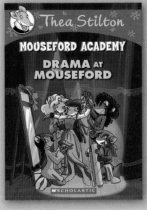

Mouseford Academy

Don't miss any of these exciting Thea Sisters adventures!

Thea Stilton and the Dragon's Code

Thea Stilton and the Mountain of Fire

Thea Stilton and the Ghost of the Shipwreck

Thea Stilton and the Secret City

Thea Stilton and the Mystery in Paris

Thea Stilton and the Cherry Blossom Adventure

Thea Stilton and the Star Castaways

Thea Stilton: Big Trouble in the Big Apple

Thea Stilton and the Ice Treasure

Thea Stilton and the Secret of the Old Castle

Thea Stilton and the Blue Scarab Hunt

Thea Stilton and the Prince's Emerald

Thea Stilton and the Mystery on the Orient Express

Thea Stilton and the Dancing Shadows

Thea Stilton and the Legend of the Fire Flowers

Thea Stilton and the Spanish Dance Mission

Thea Stilton and the
Journey to the Lion's Den

Thea Stilton and the
Great Tulip Heist

Thea Stilton and the
Chocolate Sabotage

Thea Stilton and the
Missing Myth

Thea Stilton and the
Lost Letters

Thea Stilton and the
Tropical Treasure

Thea Stilton and the
Hollywood Hoax

Thea Stilton and the
Madagascar Madness

Thea Stilton and the
Frozen Fiasco

Thea Stilton and the
Venice Masquerade

Thea Stilton and the
Niagara Splash

Thea Stilton and the
Riddle of the Ruins

Thea Stilton and the
Phantom of the Orchestra

Thea Stilton and the
Black Forest Burglary

Thea Stilton and the
Race for the Gold

Thea Stilton and the
Rainforest Rescue

Visit Geronimo in every universe!

Spacemice

Geronimo Stiltonix and his crew are out of this world!

Cavemice

Geronimo Stiltonoot, an ancient ancestor, is friends with the dinosaurs in the Stone Age!

Micekings

Geronimo Stiltonord live amongst the dragons i the ancient far north!

Don't miss any of my adventures in the Kingdom of Fantasy!

THE KINGDOM OF FANTASY

THE QUEST FOR PARADISE:
THE RETURN TO THE KINGDOM OF FANTASY

THE AMAZING VOYAGE:
THE THIRD ADVENTURE IN THE KINGDOM OF FANTASY

THE DRAGON PROPHECY:
THE FOURTH ADVENTURE IN THE KINGDOM OF FANTASY

THE VOLCANO OF FIRE:
THE FIFTH ADVENTURE IN THE KINGDOM OF FANTASY

THE SEARCH FOR TREASURE:
THE SIXTH ADVENTURE IN THE KINGDOM OF FANTASY

THE ENCHANTED CHARMS:
THE SEVENTH ADVENTURE IN THE KINGDOM OF FANTASY

THE PHOENIX OF DESTINY:
AN EPIC KINGDOM OF FANTASY ADVENTURE

THE HOUR OF MAGIC:
THE EIGHTH ADVENTURE IN THE KINGDOM OF FANTASY

THE WIZARD'S WAND:
THE NINTH ADVENTURE IN THE KINGDOM OF FANTASY

THE SHIP OF SECRETS:
THE TENTH ADVENTURE IN THE KINGDOM OF FANTASY

THE DRAGON OF FORTUNE:
AN EPIC KINGDOM OF FANTASY ADVENTURE

THE GUARDIAN OF THE REALM:
THE ELEVENTH ADVENTURE IN THE KINGDOM OF FANTASY

THE ISLAND OF DRAGONS:
THE TWELFTH ADVENTURE IN THE KINGDOM OF FANTASY

THE BATTLE FOR CRYSTAL CASTLE:
THE THIRTEENTH ADVENTURE IN THE KINGDOM OF FANTASY

Don't miss a single fabumouse adventure!

Up Next:

THANKS FOR READING, AND GOOD-BYE UNTIL OUR NEXT ADVENTURE!

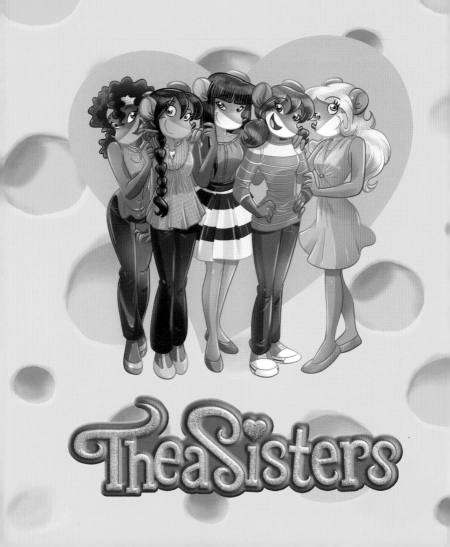